Other titles from Hodder Children's Books

The Opening Eye

heard Heaven

of Folk O

Amidships

JUPITER
Amidships

S. I. MARTIN

**Hodder
Children's
Books**

A division of Hachette Children's Books

A Catalogue record for this book is available
from the British Library

ISBN 978 0 340 98131 3

Typeset in Berkeley by Avon DataSet Ltd,
Bidford on Avon, Warwickshire

Printed in the UK by CPI Bookmarque, Croydon, CR0 4TD

The paper and board used in this paperback by Hodder Children's
Books are natural recyclable products made from wood grown in
sustainable forests. The manufacturing processes conform to the
environmental regulations of the country of origin.

Hodder Children's Books
a division of Hachette Children's Books
338 Euston Road, London NW1 3BH
An Hachette UK Company
www.hachette.co.uk

To Mom and Dad

I could not move because I was wrapped around the topmast like a python on a pig, and I'd been hanging on for dear life for at least two hours. And as I clung there, I cursed Midshipman Edward Hines and the entire Royal Navy with its petty, vicious regulations.

The sea was *definitely* too close! The ship dipped perilously low towards the sea. I couldn't believe how near I was to the water. I felt I could touch it if I stretched out an arm or a leg. Spray blew from the crests of the waves and drove across me in blinding and drenching showers.

I must have been well over one hundred feet above the main deck yet sea water splashed against my face with every dip and roll of the *Boneta*. I wasn't going to let that thought bother me. Others had done this. Sailors endured this punishment all the time in the Royal Navy. I was not going to fail. All I had to do was hold on. That was easy enough. Wasn't it?

As long as I was forced to be on this ship I would do

my best. I had not chosen to join the navy, but I could be a good sailor – I was sure of it.

Other people seem to get through life without making enemies. I wish I could overlook stupid, cruel and boring people, but I can't. They always make life harder for everyone else. Especially when they are in charge of things, and they usually are. Mr Hines has no business being a midshipman, or a 'young gentleman' as they are called. He's a year younger than me and it's only because he comes from a moneyed and connected family that he can stamp around this ship giving orders to the other men (some of whom are three times his age). Midshipman Edward Hines was the reason I was on the *Boneta* in the first place, and as if that was not bad enough he seemed to delight in making life as hard for me as possible.

This morning, he'd joined some of us new hands on the main deck to give us instruction on basic knots. He began by delivering a deeply boring and cosmically irrelevant lecture on the various forms of rope, cord and cable that had been developed and all the professions whose duties required the use of cordage. We next passed an entire hour whipping up rope and securing stray ends. Another hour was spent ensuring that the imbeciles in the group were acquainted with simple overhand knots. I am not boasting when I say that during my brief time aboard I had already managed to distinguish myself amongst the new hands. Compared to the rest of the intake, I was physically more able, had read more widely and was more numerate than average (my brother Patrick, having been to sea before, had been rated as an able seaman and was already busy aloft in the rigging of the foremast).

I suspect my education and demeanour did much to set the mood of the other hands against me. I knew I was already an object of their jokes. I'm afraid I caused the older hands a good deal of annoyance with my innumerable questions, in my eagerness to get acquainted with everything connected with the ship and my new duties. My love of clean clothes and my dislike of rum would make me few friends on this ship of smelly drunkards. Even though they nicknamed me the Black Prince, I was keen to join in and show willing where I could, and truth to tell, I was enjoying myself. I have always loved being on the water and there was so much to learn aboard the *Boneta* that I was really interested in. Almost everything fascinated me, from the names for all the rigging and yards to the routine of the watches, the ranks, the weapons . . . I felt a surge of joy rise within me as I surveyed the ship, its crew and its workings. This was something I could master. I could be very good at all of this if I set my mind to it. I had not the faintest doubt that I would succeed in all that was demanded of me. Yet deep down, I harboured a resentment against the Royal Navy because we were, in effect, prisoners on board the *Boneta*. We had been most violently kidnapped from the docks by a press gang and forced to serve on this frigate for as long as it pleased the captain. It was a sentence that could last for several years.

That morning I was hoping to discover the world of advanced casting off knots and monkey chain knots and Flemish eye knots but the fool of a midshipman informed us that an excellent way to secure sail was to employ a sheepshank knot. Now, I know I am only rated as a landman (that's what they call those of us who have never been to sea before) but I have done some sailing in river and coastal boats back in Sierra Leone. My father (may he rest in peace) taught me how to fashion knots and secure materials of all kinds. Sheepshanks are totally unsuitable for bearing loads on ocean-going vessels, and indeed for anything beyond children's games. Obviously, what the young gentleman meant to show us was a sheet bend knot as the ropes he held before him were of different sizes and strengths, but he'd confused sheep with sheet and shank with bend.

'Begging your pardon, Mr Hines,' I blurted.

Everyone on deck froze as one, then turned their heads very slowly towards me.

Mr Hines smiled at me with his mouth alone. Though I stood directly in front of him his eyes darted about me as if following a fly.

'We will hear what this young landman has to say.'

Baby Brookes, the bosun's mate, moved to my side and hooked his thumbs into his belt. He growled in my ear and bared his teeth. As he used no words whatsoever it was only some days later that I was given to understand that exchanges such as those I was about to embark on with Midshipman Hines merited extraordinary punishment under navy regulations. The young gentleman ordered the bosun's mate to stand back, all the better to assess this new threat to his authority.

'I believe you will find that knot unusable, sir.'

'How so?'

'It is a sheepshank.'

'On this matter there is no dispute.'

I ignored the laughter this comment elicited and continued. 'What is required is a bend of some sort, ideally a sheet bend.'

'How so?'

'A question of weight, sir. Allowing for adverse weather conditions, perhaps some wetness of sail and the motion of the ship on the waters, there's no sheepshank on earth that can take a strain such as you describe.'

Mr Hines nodded, appearing to digest my remarks. He cast a gaze around the crew as if inviting further comment.

'No, of course, I must disagree. How long have you been at sea, landman?'

'Four days, sir.'

'Four days. Oooh, a lifetime indeed!' The rogues on deck sneered along with him. 'Now, by way of advancing my argument,' he continued, 'I shall request the presence of our bosun's mate. Mr Brookes!'

Baby Brookes scuttled reluctantly from my side to the midshipman's, touching what would have been his forelock (had he not had African ancestry).

'Mr Brookes will now demonstrate the correct binding of a ship-shape sheepshank.' This was accomplished in under five seconds. 'And exactly how much, or what order of weight, *landman*, would you say, could such a connection sustain, and under what conditions?'

'Truth to tell, Mr Hines, it's difficult to be exact, but for use on a ship such as the *Boneta* in weather such as the master claims we're likely to meet this evening, I'd say not much over one hundred pounds of wet sail.'

Hines stroked his chin and ground his teeth as if lost in deep consideration of these variables.

'One hundred pounds, you say. What would *you* say, Mr Brookes?'

'Don't rightly know, sir,' he said, patting his invisible forelock again. 'A right goodly weight, nonetheless.'

Hines looked me up and down. 'Hmmn. A goodly weight, indeed. Bind this young man from head to foot, bosun's mate! And secure it all with your tightest sheepshank, if you please.'

Before I could voice my shock, a web of cord had been spun about me, passed twice between my legs, once over each shoulder and pulled firm. The securing knot at my waist was tighter than I'd have thought possible for a sheepshank.

'All hands hold to, now!' the midshipman commanded. The forest of grins which greeted this order confirmed my fear that I had not one true friend on board this ship of ruffians save my brother Patrick. 'Pass the rope over the yardarm. Sharply, now!'

The rope end was flung over the mizzen mast's yardarm and I began to fear for my life. Stories about sailors being tortured to death were not uncommon.

'Haul one, haul all,' came the cry. I was pulled up, kicking desperately into the air above the deck, with all my weight being carried by my waist.

'Let's be floggin' that darkie, now, jes' like we do in Jamaikee!' whooped a wild new sailor.

Swift, harsh looks from the two senior crew members on deck silenced him into shrivelled embarrassment.

'Now, Landman Williams, how is this? Is this a suitable knot or not for a weighty ship-borne load?'

Tight though it was, I sensed that the knot could slip loose given sufficient rough teasing from the deckhands, so I told him, by way of shaking my head in terror, that the knot was far from secure.

'Not made fast enough?' crowed the young gentleman in mock-amazement, as if he was a conjuror on stage. 'Shake that sheepshank, lads. Let's see you shake all the sheet and bends out of the fellow. Shake away, now! Shake!'

My bound body was raised almost to the yardarm and lowered roughly to the deck repeatedly with increasing speed and violence. To compound my misery the deckhands sang a little shanty.

'They call me hanging Johnnie
Hooray, hooray,
They call me hanging Johnnie
Hang, boys, hang

They said I hanged for money,
Hooray, hooray,
But I never hanged nobody,
Hang, boys, hang

I'd hang a noted liar,
Hooray, hooray,
I'd hang a bloated friar,
Hang, boys, hang

I'd hang a brutal mother,
Hooray, hooray,
I'd hang her and no other,
Hang, boys, hang

I'd hang to make things jolly
Hooray, hooray,
I'd hang all wrong and folly,
Hang, boys, hang

They call me hanging Johnnie
Hooray, hooray,
They call me hanging Johnnie
Hang, boys, hang.'

After I'd crashed to the deck for the eighth time, the midshipman came to kneel beside me. He removed his hat and wiped his brow. 'So tell me now, in your considered opinion, Landman Williams, is the sheepshank a knot you would use to fasten sail and other loads on board this ship?'

Racked with every imaginable physical pain, I nodded.

'And shall I take that to mean "yes" in your language, landman?'

'Aye, aye, sir,' I croaked.

'Aloft with the wretched fellow, Mr Brookes, and bind him fast to the crow's nest!'

I was pulled towards the sky again. 'Let the wind and water be his tutor tonight. And, landman,' he walked underneath me and stared into my face, 'mind your tongue and be thankful I've not awarded you the lashes you so richly deserve!'

So here I am hours later stuck at the ship's highest point, in the wind and rain, and commanded to remain here at the pleasure of my newest enemy: Midshipman Hines.

There was no rigging up here suitable for hooking my elbows through, so I used my belt to strap myself to the mast. And as I had already loosened the main knot of my restraints (which Baby Brookes had been thoughtful enough to leave within reach of my fingers) I made myself both safe and comfortable.

I suffer from neither seasickness nor a fear of heights, but this topmast torment combined the very worst elements of both these conditions. On top of everything else, I had to face my biggest fear: boredom. After studying the patterns made by families of rats being chased by the ship's ferret through the rigging there was nothing to do. There was nowhere to put my mind – except inwards to my miserable reflections or out, far out to sea . . .

After another hour I fixed my gaze on the masts of the other ships in our little convoy. There were four other frigates. They travelled with us in a diamond formation with our ship at the centre. But I've no idea what our purpose is or where we are bound. All I can conclude is that we are somewhere in the Atlantic Ocean. I wonder if our course will take us near Africa?

Since stepping on board the *Boneta* I've been trying to overhear and make sense of every conversation I can. Rumours abound on a ship like this. Baby Brookes, the bosun's mate, says we 'be bound for Afrikee for dobbing the Sallee Rovers one on', whatever that means. I've also heard the master and ship's officers cursing the large, inconveniently placed crane that stands above the hold. Because I visit the hold daily as part of my delivery duties, I know it is also home to Dr Belloni, a very strange Italian gentleman. I've glimpsed him tinkering with some apparatus which keeps him permanently below decks. What its purpose is I cannot imagine. Some say we are on a secret mission, that they've never sailed on such a closely guarded ship with marines stationed at every single hatchway. But I couldn't care about secret missions. I only hoped that we really were on the way to Africa. I hadn't seen my home in Sierra Leone in almost four years. I could barely remember what it looked like.

At the top of the ship every motion is amplified. I can feel everything up here. The ropes rattle noisily, the sound mingling with the flapping ends of loosened sails beating against their yards. Every ripple feels like a rolling wave and the slightest dip a plunge. From so high above the deck everything looks extraordinary. I started to notice the wildly different colours of the waters. Some were blue, some were black, others blue-black and grey edging into cobalt and colours without names. Colours which were all colours and none. I could have sworn that in places the sea was transparent and for a while I felt as if I had left my body and was rising above the convoy to look down upon it. There were shapes under the waves. Not just shapes, but ghostly lights as well. The scene they illuminated was magical. I could discern underwater mountains and valleys. And were those really underwater castles and villages and the carriages of merfolk that I saw trundling up and down them? Eventually I grew increasingly lightheaded, until I was almost convinced that everything – the sea, the night – was unreal; that I was the victim of a particularly bad nightmare; and that I would soon wake to find myself safely in my hammock under the glow of the swinging mess lamps. It was the fear of my growing insanity that shocked me back to reality.

I must have been strapped to the mainmast for at least four hours because I heard the bell ring to change the watches on deck. I should have been with my messmates by now. They would be nice and warm, or at least dry below decks. Very soon I again lost all sense of perspective.

Then it started to rain. Those on watch now wore oilskins. They paced to and fro seeking shelter when they could under the boats stowed on the booms. The clean, new set of clothes in which I left London three weeks ago were ripped, stiff and marked with layers of sweat and sea spray.

I hadn't eaten since breakfast and my sense of time decreased as my hunger grew. The smell of salt beef and plum duff boiling rose up from below decks, and I imagined little Francis toiling away beside the fat cook in the tiny galley, bashing canvas bags full of broken biscuits and rolling and cutting out stiff dough.

I tried to keep track of the various bells – sixteen bells sounded twice. That meant that eight hours have passed, I think. Or did it mean it was four in the morning? On the quarterdeck a knot of marines with fixed bayonets were staring up at me in an unusually relaxed manner. I guessed they had been laying bets on how long I'd survive up here.

Across from them the usual group of middle-ranking bullies foregathered beside the lee rail. One of them I could clearly see was Mr Hines. He glanced up at me, studied his fob-watch and carefully relit his pipe in the wet environment.

Suddenly, I saw my older brother Patrick waving across to me from his usual post halfway up the foremast, where he was adjusting a stretch of rigging. I still get confused about the different masts and sails and cannot yet tell a gaff peak halliard from a mizzen-topgallant halliard. I couldn't see if Patrick was smiling or not. He was clenching his fist, but it wasn't in greeting. He was swinging his arm in a long, low underarm motion. He was holding slingshot. It was weighted with a small package. It came flying across to me. I was too dazed to catch it, but it connected with my forehead, and thus dropped safely and neatly at my feet. It was a small bundle of ship's biscuit and cheese. I hate cheese, so I threw it into the sea immediately after my brother had climbed down from his mast and was out of sight. I tapped the biscuit to dislodge an army of tiny beetles and munched merrily.

I stared out into the black night; the shrouded deck below me had fallen silent and was now almost deserted except for the steady tramp of the lookouts from rail to rail calling from one to another 'All's well' from deck to deck.

I don't have a clue where we are, though obviously

we are not in enemy waters as I can remain up here in the lookout for so many watches. There was no coastline to guide my intuition. I knew next to nothing about the positions of the stars. I imagined I could discern the Plough . . . or was that the Great Bear or the Hunter? My little brother Robert would have known. He could have told me exactly were we were, how fast we were travelling, where we were going and when we'd get there. He had tried to teach me a little astronomy once when we were at school in London. But I have no head for navigation. All I really want is to get back home to Freetown, Sierra Leone and I don't care which star guides me there.

[2]

I opened my eyes to a dark, lowering morning. The desolate sea was still threateningly rough. Heavy clouds hung low. A hand was at my shoulder.

' 'Tain't likely you'll be looking to fix folds abaft or hove in all the cargee, heh-heh. I'll lay to that! Hold fast to me.' It was the voice of Baby Brookes: a voice that could have come from Panama, Poplar or Port-of-Spain. Apart from the last four words I hadn't understood a word the bosun's mate said, but I replied: 'Aye!!' and laughed like I imagined a true seaman would. I held tightly on to him as he untied me then threw me over his shoulders like a sack and carried me down the mast. This was no mean feat, as I am no lightweight and he was only slightly larger than me. They called him Baby Brookes because he was actually born on board the *Boneta*. His mother was one of the 'wives' of a particularly depraved captain. Baby has lived on this ship his entire life. No one knows his first name. As an infant, he was entered in the ship's records simply as *Baby*. The name stuck.

The *Boneta* is his entire world.

A roar like a bull being roasted alive reverberated through the *Boneta* from somewhere beneath the main deck. All the deckhands were rendered immobile by the sound. Only when it stopped did I notice that all eyes were upon me. They were grinning unkindly. Then I remembered . . . Exhaustion, sleeplessness and cold aside, there was another matter I had to face that morning which set me quaking with terror. I would be brought face to face with the captain of the *Boneta* that morning in a most terrible way.

The unholy noise tore through the ship a second time. 'God be with you, young'un,' muttered an old sailor as he passed. 'Captain Hibbert has the rage of the damned today!'

The lure of sleep was pressing greatly upon me, but I had tasks to perform. I had vowed from my first step aboard this ship that I would never disgrace myself or bring shame upon my family or my people. I shook myself into greater wakefulness and set to my duties.

The worst jobs on every ship always go to the new hands. I have never been lucky when it comes to lotteries, so I was unsurprised to end up with manger duty. The manger is a low shed tucked under the poopdeck. Inside it a cow, two pigs, four hens, and a goat are stalled. They produce eggs, milk, meat and manure in abundance. Like most new sailors I was shocked to find livestock quartered away aboard a Royal Navy vessel, baaing, mooing and pooing as if in the wilds of Wiltshire. I had to tend to them. We all know what that means. These creatures generate animal waste in copious quantities. One of my tasks is to dispose of this. I also milk the cow, collect the eggs and make the area a fit place for them to endure another day and night in.

I feel I'm good at the mucking out and deliveries now even if I'm still soaked through to the skin and shivering like a ghost.

As if I didn't have enough enemies in human form, I have another in the manger. His name is Lucifer: a goat. He charges at me whenever I approach the stable, seeking to deny me entry. What purpose a goat serves on one of King George's ships I will never know. Lucifer is clearly male. He can produce no milk and is too old for tender meat after slaughter. I sometimes think he has been put on deck by the Almighty to add to my tests and torments. I am obliged to fight with the beast on a daily basis as he attempts to deny me access to the manger through the use of his horns. The technique I am perfecting involves draping my coat over his horns and face as he comes at me, then kicking his flanks severely to disorient him before flinging a noose about his neck and hauling him to the farthest point of the pen.

As usual, Lucifer came at me, without mercy.

The first thing I did after wrestling Lucifer into the corner was to get some milk down my throat. After a couple of weeks at sea I can now tell which beast needs milking first. I was so tired and crushed of spirit that I slid myself under the first cow I came to. With open mouth under the cow's teat I started to milk upside down. I drank long and deep of the fresh milk. I drank till my spirits were steadied and I came to my senses. Using a strip of panelling and a leather bucket, I scooped away the worst of the waste then gathered up an armful of clean straw. It was alive with rats, so I threw it to the deck and stamped on it till they perished or fled.

The *Boneta* is what is known as a ratty ship. This is not a good thing. The rats are everywhere. A ratty ship is one whose human occupants are vastly outnumbered by those of large, stinky, glue-furred, long-tailed, rodent origin. We have rats in the rigging, rats in the galley, rats in the hold, wardroom rats, bilge rats, captain's rats, master's rats, topsail rats, taffrail rats, hammock rats, cheese rats, cheesy-toe rats, biscuit rats, salt-beef rats, rum rats, salt rats and rat-eating rats. I mostly deal with manger rats. They eat the husks, rinds, old biscuit and sour beer we feed the animals. They eat the animals too. All the beasts bear bite-marks. A ship's legend tells of how one of the new midshipmen went missing on a night watch. His corpse was found two days later in a corner of the hold. The vermin had made a cosy home for themselves in what they'd left of his body.

I distributed the straw about the manger and set about milking. I slapped a pail under the beast whose milk I had just drunk, squatted down and tried to milk her. I was too tired and woke up some minutes later with a shiver, realizing I'd fallen asleep with my head against the cow's flank.

Feeling the slide towards sleep pull anew, I jerked myself back into the milking position and began the work in earnest, booting the odd inquisitive, milk-loving rat away as I worked.

Having filled four small churns with rich, clean, warm milk, I singled out that which I'd present to the midshipmen's mess. Into this I spat severely and swilled the resultant mess about with an unwashed forefinger.

I strewed the clean straw about the place and booted it into presentable positions. There was only the feeding to do now and that was easy. After a couple of invigorating runs down to the galley and back I slopped generous measures of mouldy ship's biscuit, old husks, older rusks, sour beer and filthy porridge into their troughs and left them to get on with it amongst the rats.

Carrying four heavy churns full of milk and a bag of fresh eggs up and down the ladders and hatchways of a frigate is *not* easy work. As I rank amongst the lowest of the low, I'm obliged to give way to almost everyone else I happen to share a passageway with.

The one crew member who will never allow me to give way, or who will never give way to me is Sergeant Mills of the marines. He is a grey-chopped, red-eyed swine who has made it his business to terrorize every black man on the *Boneta*. That is a lot of terrorizing, and he excels at it. In common with some of the crew, Mills spent some of his army service in Jamaica. Apparently some bad things happened to him there which caused him to turn against all sons and daughters of Africa. He stalks the corridors and hatchways of the *Boneta* like a ghost. At all times he carries a knout in his fist, that is to say he swings a dirty, short, tarred length of knotted rope. He uses this implement to lash out at any black crew member he happens upon. He strikes all the black crew as a matter of course, not to say as a matter of principle. That morning he caught me as I was hurrying to the captain's cabin. He had lain in wait for me as I bobbed through the hatchway. The knout caught me on my forehead, above my right eye. It hurt, and I think it drew some little blood. But I could not stop. I had too much to do.

'Don't forget, the captain wants to see you after your duties,' Sergeant Mills growled.

I was let into Captain Hibbert's dining cabin by a marine sentry. Francis was already busy in there cleaning up breakfast cutlery. It was always difficult seeing Francis. Patrick and I had known him for less than two months, yet in that time we had experienced much together, including my flight from school in London, nearly being sold into slavery and our capture and imprisonment by the press gang. I had hoped he would join us on our eventual journey to Sierra Leone, but from the moment he stepped aboard the *Boneta* there was a change in his mood and manners. Like me, he liked life at sea, but unlike me Africa had no meaning for him. He had found his home.

'You really don't look for an easy life, do you, Jupiter?'

I scowled at that short bushy-haired young child that I had dragged, yes, *physically dragged* from bondage. He shook his head at me as if he was some grey-bearded know-it-all. He has adapted well to life at sea and has the most undemanding tasks as usual. He helps the chef and he serves the captain ready-mashed and nibble-sized food at his table. He is almost like a ship's mascot. I was just readying myself to cuff him when he turned back into the room and threw me a twist of salt cod and a nice fat half-lime which he motioned me to pocket.

'Good luck with Captain Hibbert, Jupiter. And whatever he says or does to you, don't take it personally.'

But I would take it personally. I was about to enter into a situation with the captain that, apart from actual intimacy, was as personal as could be imagined. I wolfed the fish and lime long before I'd reached my next stop: the midshipman's berth.

The door to the young gentlemen's berth was opened by the Honourable Mr Collett. *Young gentlemen indeed!* The room was dominated by an ancient table, on to which were carved the names of previous diners. One midshipman was a child aged ten or eleven, and another seemed younger still judging by his size and manners. I was surprised not to see brightly coloured building blocks, wheeled toys and fluffy quadrupeds spilling across their mess. Mr Hines was not amongst them, much to my relief, but I had an idea of where he could be found.

'Here he is! Hail our young rig rat!' cried the Honourable Mr Collett. 'He's looking none the worse for wear. Say, blackie, I reckon you've made me a good ten shillings from our old chum Eddie.'

Their 'old chum Eddie' was none other than Mr Hines. Collett was an even less competent seaman than him, but somewhat better connected. His father is something like a lord or a baron. He'll probably be an admiral within ten years. There are a lot like him in the navy.

'Eddie can afford to lose a few shillings,' hollered a young man swinging in a hammock. 'Money means nothing to him!'

'Then he has no shame. Though I'm sure Jupiter, our Black Prince here, could make him blush, eh? That would be a first!'

I saw no reason to respond to this sort of jest, so I

left the milk and backed silently out towards the door before it developed into something more objectionable.

'I say, landman.' Mr Collett held a fruit in front of him. 'Would you say this mango was ripe enough to eat?'

I was almost totally ignorant about the islands of the Caribbean and their produce. In fact, it was the first time I had ever seen a mango. It smelled delicious.

'I wouldn't know anything at all about that, Mr Collett. Now, begging your pardon, I must be on my way.'

Most of these so-called *young gentlemen* are really pampered little brutes. They eat well only on account of Mr Hines. There is a rumour that he has an unearned income in excess of two thousand pounds every year. It is his money that buys the fresh milk, fresh eggs, molasses, salt beef and limes that they stuff their faces with. Not to mention the clean towels, tooth powder and blocks of French soap. But they still mock him behind his back even as they swig his good rum and make free with his small library of pocket-sized books. I slipped a small flask of coconut oil into my pocket on my way out. I would work it into my stiff, dry hair later.

* * *

Hollering my approach, I shoved past the armed marine slouching against the side-door of the hold. As I expected, Mr Hines was in there with Dr Belloni. The midshipman looked me up and down while nodding his head and grinding his teeth.

'A-ha! And how is our Black Prince this fine morning?'

As usual, Hines was dressed very well. He was the best-dressed member of this or any other crew in the Royal Navy. It wasn't simply a case of his white waistcoat, breeches and stockings being clean. Nobody's linen looked that clean. Cleaned clothes didn't have such a lustrous quality. Mr Hines's clothes always looked *new*. He had the typical voice of a midshipman: a sharp beseeching bark. Only his face seemed out of place in the middies' mess. It was black. Or at least light brown. He clearly had a parent of African origin. His skin was pitted as if he had survived smallpox. Patrick had told me of black midshipmen, surgeons and even black captains in the Royal Navy, but to tell the truth I did not believe him and I certainly had not expect to encounter one on our first voyage as seamen. Normally, being under the command of a junior officer of African heritage would have been something I'd have taken pride in (not to say marvelled at) but this particular young gentleman is uniquely unlikeable. They say he is the son of a Jamaican planter. Apparently he inherited a considerable fortune upon his father's death. When in England he lives in a sumptuous apartment in Pall Mall. He has never returned to Jamaica. Nobody has the faintest idea why he has chosen a life at sea, as it seems most midshipmen have either been sent to sea for want of a fortune or are from families that have fallen from grace.

What his story is, I could not imagine.

[*3*]

It happened like this.

Back in London, I had it all planned out. I had arranged places for Patrick, Francis and myself on a merchant ship heading down to Freetown, Sierra Leone. We should be on our way home – we could even be there now, basking in the warmth of Africa's sun – had it not been for my slowness and idiocy. Instead we are in word and very deed prisoners of His Majesty King George.

When I say that our situation is my fault, I mean that we had just been allotted places on the merchant ship *Gadfly*, and were on our way to number ourselves amongst its crew when disaster befell us. Following our guide down an alleyway we fell into the clutches of a press gang hunting for sailors. *That* was all my fault.

Patrick and Francis were walking and conversing with the merchant ship's guide some yards ahead of me. I was gazing up at the walls of the streets and passages we were crossing and wondering why there were fewer and fewer street signs when we found ourselves in an alley hard by the docks. A shout went out: 'Hurrah there! Stand fast, in the name of the King!' Whereupon Patrick launched himself down the nearest alley. Francis, whose collar was in my brother's fist, flew behind him. I, on the other hand, was rooted to the spot. I found myself unable to move because I was transfixed by a sight I had hitherto thought unimaginable. Standing before me, in command of a team of English bullies, was an immaculately dressed black midshipman. He was real. This was not the figure of half-remembered fantasy with which the older Jamaican seamen regaled us in Sierra Leone, the way they told us about duppies and rolling calves. No, this shiny-shoed, glinty-buckled and buttoned-down individual was a real, living, breathing black midshipman in the Royal Navy. I could see the anchor sewn in gold thread on his collar and sleeves. He stood before me with arms outstretched, barring my way down this nameless dockside approach.

'Well, hello, *friend seafarer*,' he growled.

I was on the point of informing him that I was not, in fact, a sailor or his friend when I remembered that I was dressed in the latest maritime fashions from head to foot.

His grin was wrong. Perhaps his terrible teeth gave him away but his smile that day said, *and now you die* rather than *welcome*. I looked over his shoulder. My brother and Francis were nowhere to be seen.

With a sharp blast on a whistle, he conjured a host of rough, sour-reeking men who had been lurking in adjoining alleys. 'Seize him!' he said. 'There's another unlucky soul for the *Boneta*.'

I fought that day as well as I have ever fought. I knocked three of the brutes senseless and made my mark on a few of the rest, but I was hugely outnumbered and beaten down with bludgeons until I lost consciousness. When I came to I saw that I was bound and trussed like a deer on the cobbles. I was not alone either. Patrick and Francis were beside me, restrained in a more kindly manner.

'Patrick, what are you doing here? I thought you had made good your escape.'

'We had, Jupiter, but we came back to look for you. We couldn't leave without you, could we?' He glared at me with a ferocity I had forgotten he possessed. 'Why did you not run?' he asked, not entirely containing his rage.

'Aaah, he came back for his little brother,' crooned the black midshipman. 'How sweet! Brothers in bondage. They can serve together with the other one. Three unlucky souls for the *Boneta*!'

We were robbed and immediately imprisoned in an alehouse anteroom where we were obliged to sleep on deal planks. Throughout that night we heard our captors boasting drunkenly of their success at capturing seamen. As we listened to them singing songs that declaimed their eminent cruelty to man, woman and beast, Patrick reached over and slapped me loudly enough for the sound to echo in the wooden chamber. 'Jupiter.' He was almost choking on his words. 'You have always been the fastest runner in our family, in truth the fleetest man afoot I have ever known. Why, oh why did you not run?' As I had nothing to say, he kicked me for good measure.

Over the next two days we were marched down to Gravesend, in Kent. We were forced at bayonet-point on to an old unmasted hulk that had once served as a French flagship. Here we joined a host of unfortunates who had also fallen into the hands of the press gangs. This was a place of intense misery.

In order to avoid going to sea, some prisoners pretended they were imbeciles. but a blow to the head from the butt of a musket soon brought them to their senses. Other impressed men used copper coins to rub their small cuts into festering wounds, thus making themselves unfit for service. One fellow (an outstanding actor) bit his own tongue and feigned a fever with foaming blood oozing from between his gnashing teeth and flecking his lips. Again, considerable violence rendered him sensible. We remained in the hold of the hulk for an immeasurable length of time, day and night being meaningless in that unlit space. My strongest memory is of Patrick calling me over to his side in a pained voice. 'My brother, you should have run when you had the chance. You should have run. You should have run!' Because he is my older brother, I allowed him to strike me. He struck me three times: once on each occasion that a verb appeared in his admonition.

After a seeming eternity, those of us who were to join the *Boneta* were separated and marched en masse to our new home. Our spirits were bitter exceedingly as we were prodded aboard, four abreast, over the narrow gangplank. Dragging our feet we were halted on the forward deck where we had the first chance to view our fellow impressed seamen in daylight. Most of them were sober and silent. I confess I was surprised to see so few mean or vicious faces and to hear so little blasphemy and bad language. Their faces told the simple stories of their former lives; the farm labourer, the trawlerman, the clerk, the footman, now all on one common level of misfortune and misery. They were not criminals at all, but like us, merely unlucky men, torn from their comforts and trapped in a situation beyond their control.

The instant the black midshipman had turned his back on us to address another party, Patrick, who was standing beside me, jabbed me violently in the ribs. 'Welcome to Hell, Jupiter,' he hissed. He had been to sea before and was a good seaman. There was no reason to doubt his judgement. 'Thank you for delivering us to this ocean-going jail,' he sneered. 'What is wrong with you, my brother? Why did you not take to your heels? Oh, you fool. You should have run!' As I expected he would, he punctuated his speech with blows to my body.

Over the past two weeks the young black midshipman has certainly made good his promise to teach every man jack of us 'the dread of the yardarm' and the 'horrors of the forepeak'! We may not be learning seamanship of the most accurate kind, but we are certainly learning quickly.

* * *

The entire hold was fogged with tobacco fumes. The volume of smoke was incredible. For both the seaman and the scientist, to breathe was to smoke. Hines had his teeth clamped about his clay pipe as often as possible and Belloni swallowed smoke from the nastiest cheroots. The only other light in the space came from what looked like a large jar of fireflies. Hines seemed to spend every morning down here with Belloni. They were talking together over a set of diagrams in what I took to be Italian. Apart from a trailing comprehension of spoken French, I have no facility with languages and I am always amazed to hear an English speaker twist up their mouths without apparent hesitation. Hines and Belloni both wore belted aprons ringed with a great many tiny tools and pockets. The hold was divided by a screen which shielded some huge mechanical object from general perusal. Apart from my overwhelming wish that evil should befall the midshipman, I had no interest whatsoever in their business. I would dump the milk churn and be gone before my temper got the better of me.

The midshipman looked up from his papers and, using head movements alone, directed me down into the corridor out of the marine sentry's sight and hearing. If he harboured any ideas of personally inflicting further punishments upon me in this narrow space, he was very much mistaken. I was heavier and taller than he was. Throughout my night aloft I had kept myself warm by stoking the fires of revenge in my heart with dreams of the unholy cruelty I would unleash upon this individual should the opportunity present itself.

Now here we were, face to face, in the dark bowels of the *Boneta*. Hines had an apron full of tinker-tools. I had a weighty churn full of milk in my fist. I was imagining the sound it would make as it bounced off his head four or five times when he blurted: 'Stand easy, landman.' He scrutinized me as if he was a doctor and I his patient. 'You appear to be no worse for your night among the stars.'

I grunted, adding 'sir' reluctantly. I began to swing the churn very slowly from side to side.

'I'll come to the point.' He thrust his face closer. 'You think I was somewhat hard on you, don't you?' he snapped.

'I do, Mr Hines,' I snapped back, ready to support my position with facts or fists as his response demanded.

'You feel I was overly severe perhaps?'

I nodded. There was a tone in his voice that I could

not identity. It was as if he was mocking me. I braced myself to my full height and squared my shoulders. If he was trying to provoke me he might just succeed beyond his wildest dreams.

'Maybe you are aggrieved that I, as a fellow son of Africa, would so ill-use another? You are very wrong, Jupiter. I know what sort of fellow you are. You have unusual resilience. A stormy night at the topmast wouldn't even give a man such as yourself a head cold. Well, it hasn't, has it? You don't even have the sniffles, nary a wisp of nasal drip. You are as tough as old boots, man.' He punched me on the shoulder in a most unofficer-like manner. 'Jupiter, I did you a *favour*. Do you understand that?'

'Then, sir, if I may venture to be so bold, if last night was an example of how you dispense favours I would not wish any man to be subject to your ill humour.'

Hines hooted with laughter and clapped twice. 'Funny fellow. Yet still you grasp neither my motivations nor the workings of the King's navy. Listen, I am a midshipman. I am, moreover, a man of ambition. One in my position cannot be made the laughing stock of any ship. My authority cannot be thwarted in so public a fashion as you—'

'My intention was merely to establish the—'

'That is beside the point. I cannot let a slight to my authority pass unpunished. Even if you are right and I am wrong. This is the Royal Navy. *I. Outrank. You.* I command. You obey. Either I had to be seen to punish you, or endure the rest of my naval career under a cloud of shame.' He shook his head. 'With a few exceptions, the crew of this good ship are, for the large part, morons who could not draw a straight line in the snow with their own piss.'

I tried not to laugh, but what he said was true.

'I need them on my side, if I'm to advance my career. What better way to keep in their good books than to allow them to administer a small dose of rough justice on my behalf.'

Somehow, I felt as though the chance of clouting Hines with the churn had passed.

'I was faced with the choice of awarding you a flogging of several dozen lashes (which, believe me, you merited) or an instant punishment of my own devising. Which would you have preferred?'

He had given me nothing to consider. I had seen the monstrous, ridged scars that Patrick still carried on his back from a lesser flogging over two years ago. I knew that a flogging often resulted in infections and sometimes death for stronger men than myself. What

Midshipman Hines had subjected me to was but a mere stroll in the foothills of Mount Pain.

'And what's more,' he continued, 'you are now a champion of sorts amongst the men. No longer the haughty Black Prince. You have become, dare I say it, *one of the lads*. The officers think highly of you too, in spite of your strange ways. I will have you understand that I fully intend to make the rank of captain before any of my fellow midshipmen, and one of my birth,' he pinched the skin on his cheek, 'cannot possibly be seen to favour one race of men over any other, can he? I'll thank you for the doctor's milk now, Jupiter.' He grabbed the churn from me. 'And I look forward to seeing you on the morrow. I'll be with you once more to show you the ropes again, as it were, heh-heh. We'll be gammoning the bowsprit. You'll like that.' He laughed and slapped me on the back in a most ungentlemanly fashion. 'You aren't as clever as you think, Jupiter,' he called after me, 'but you're much wiser than you know, you know. Hurry along now. It won't do to keep the captain waiting, heh-heh.'

I was most glad to be away from that quarter of the ship. Tobacco smoke notwithstanding, Belloni is a supernaturally smelly person. Apart from ship's biscuits and milk he eats only spoonfuls of sloppy, malodorous Italian cheese and slices of hard-looking sausage. The stench in the hold certainly gave substance to the rumour that he never left it for *any* reason.

I found myself lost in consideration of what exactly 'gammoning the bowsprit' could entail when the ship shook once more with the captain's strangled scream.

The captain's howls could still be heard above the noise of the sea and the shouts of the hands on deck and in the rigging.

As well as managing the manger and being trained daily in the rigging with the other landmen, I am also a loblolly boy. I assist the ship's surgeon when needed. What this means is that because I am stronger and younger than average I am expected to hold down struggling patients on the doctor's operating table. My full title is 'surgeon's mate', which means I also get to throw hacked-off limbs and body parts into a bucket. I'm relied on to dispose of the dead (mercifully there have been and will be none of those on this voyage).

Dr Druce was waiting for me at the threshold of the wardroom. 'Where the devil have you been, boy? You should have been here at two bells sharp.' Without waiting to hear my answer he grabbed my waistcoat and dragged me inside. 'Come now, to work. The captain can't wait all day.'

Captain Maurice Hibbert glowered at me most

evilly. He was fighting a ceaseless battle against a monstrous toothache which threatened to destroy him, body and soul, as it fixed its claws ever more firmly upon his jaw. His cheeks were puffed out in the effort of gargling and groaning at the same time. I was so petrified by the brutality of the captain's expression that it was a while before I noticed that a young Scottish seaman whose name I could not recall was also in the room with us. He gave me a wink and a smile as if to indicate we were 'all in this thing together'. We were not though. I knew the role I had to play. I had no idea at all what he was doing there.

'Captain, sir?' The doctor steered the captain to a porcelain bowl. 'You may now spit it out.'

Captain Hibbert released a mouthful of rich yellow liquid. Its familiar smell startled me. I stared at it in appalled fascination and shot a deeply questioning glance at the doctor.

'*Yes, it is!*' he mouthed, raising his eyebrows in emphasis.

'Now, if we are all quite ready,' said the captain, 'let's get this wretched business over with as quickly as possible!' He stretched himself out on the table. Dr Druce unrolled a set of dental instruments so diabolical that a slave master would have been ashamed to own them. They were chipped, rough-hewn and wrapped in canvas that was speckled with ages-old dried blood. Understandably, there was little demand for Druce's brand of dentistry on the *Boneta*.

'Now, Seaman Sclater!' The surgeon wielded a rusty wrench. 'Let's get that nice, clean, fat young tooth out of your skull. After that, I shall remove Captain Hibbert's bad tooth and replace it with your good one. And let us not forget, the sum of two shillings that you will earn for your pains. Open wide!'

The young Scotsman jumped to the doctor's orders and stood at ease before him. I looked on in amazement as one of the poor man's back teeth was rocked and popped out of his head. Sclater did not so much as grunt during the five minutes this operation took.

'Yes, this will do very nicely.' The doctor looked, sniffed it and placed it carefully in a china dish. 'An excellent specimen, I think you'll agree, captain.'

'Just hurry up, for God's sake, man!' moaned Captain Hibbert.

'Yes, sir, of course. Your turn now; open wide, if you please.'

I stood at the head of the table and held the captain's shoulders down securely.

'Able Seaman Sclater has already demonstrated how little pain is involved in this operation. It won't take long.'

Using the same unwashed instrument that had been in the junior seaman's mouth just moments before, the surgeon went to work on the captain's rotten tooth.

I looked away, not wishing to witness the anguish of another human being, especially one whose breath smelled like a bucket of dead toads.

'*Yawrafrookarooka!*' the captain screamed as he tried to head-butt the surgeon. '*Hrooschl ya frookarooka shwerkli!*'

I was having a hard job keeping the captain on the table. He was not a big man, but his pain had empowered him with the strength of ten. He wriggled from my hold, batted Druce away and snatched the wrench from him. 'Get away from me, you torturer!' He threatened Dr Druce with the instrument. 'You're as weak as Welsh tea. My grandmother could pull a tooth faster, and she's been dead many a year.'

'But it's not a whole tooth, captain,' protested the surgeon. 'It has been worn down almost to the gum. There's precious little left to grip. It is tender work.'

Captain Hibbert snarled at him. 'Tender work! Bah! You!' He beckoned me forwards with the wrench. 'You do it. You pull it out. Sharply now!'

'Why, captain, he's but a boy, a loblolly lad. He has no skills in medi—' The captain silenced him with a bloodshot glare.

'He will do it. And he will do it now or I'll clap the Negro in irons and sell his black hide to the Turks.'

It is not in my nature to shirk from a challenge, but I confess there was more confidence in my step than my touch as I strode forward and grasped the wrench.

'Open wide,' I said. The captain yawned and once again I was assailed by a gust of breath so impossibly evil that I was nearly brought to my knees. But I prevailed and stood firm. I had an extraction to perform. Elbowing Dr Druce aside, I went to his medicine cabinet and grabbed his half-empty bottle of brandy. The captain was known to be a heavy drinker (mainly of rum, seeing as he was from a Jamaican planter family) and I was sure the measure of drink I was proposing would be less than his daily charge of strong drink for luncheon alone. With my back to him, I sprinkled a pinch of opium into the bottle, the better to sedate him.

'Captain Hibbert, I will require that you swallow this draught. In its entirety.'

'*In its entirety*, you say? So you're a scholar then?

45

You must be the one they are calling the Black Prince. You have a sober enough face, though. Pass me the brandy, let me drink, then go to it, my boy, like you were cutting cane in Clarendon.'

Holding my breath I examined the state of the tooth. It was a mess of puddled blood, crud and decomposing food in a crushed fort of brutalized enamel surrounded by swollen green gums, purple palate and the fattest, whitest tongue possible on a human being. I would need tools. Dr Druce hovered about me like a concerned fly but I ignored him. I knew exactly what I had to do. The moment the bottle rolled to the floor I was ready with my scalpel and the surgical scissors. With one knee in the captain's chest, I suddenly fixed him to the table with my full weight. His mouth was now open in shock and I flew in. It took three deft slices and two snips to reveal the greater base of the tooth. Before he could cough blood into my face, I tugged the wrench from the surgeon, made it fast around what remained of the tooth and jerked upwards. The errant molar left his mouth instantly. A gasp of relief exited the captain's body.

'You've done it, boy. You've actually done it. The horrid old gnasher is gone. Praise be! You've done it!'

'It was nothing, sir,' I said as I handed tools over

to Dr Druce. 'The ship's surgeon will now conclude the operation . . . but if I might just make one suggestion . . .'

He nodded.

'Perhaps a draught or three of the same good Spanish brandy this evening and first thing tomorrow morning would aid somewhat both in sleep and in the composition of your daily logs.'

'Capital idea,' he concurred. 'Capital!'

The ship's surgeon ushered me towards the door with a gesture that was curiously both anxious and reassuring.

'You boy! Black Prince!' called Captain Hibbert. 'How do they call you? What's your name?'

'I go by the name of Jupiter, sir. Jupiter Williams.'

'Jupiter, eh?' He stroked his chin. 'Jupiter, by Jove!'

I laughed appreciatively as if I had not heard that joke a thousand times before.

[*5*]

'Bad luck unto them I say boys,
Bad luck to them I say;
They broke into me sea chest
And they stole me clothes away.'

The singing of that dire sea-shanty stirred me to life. I woke up under a chain-table that my messmates had lowered to hide me should the bosun's crew come looking. How I've learned to sleep on this ship I'll never know, but I was feeling wonderfully refreshed, probably due to not lying shoulder to shoulder with these rogues in our hammocks and inhaling their exhalations as I do night after night.

My morning meal had been saved for me: dolphin and dumpling stew. It had gone cold and was so set in jelly that I could not distinguish dumpling from dolphin by sight or taste.

Normally I allow the others to share my rum ration. Like all other hands, I am entitled to a full half pint of this spirit every day on top of endless draughts of beer.

Why such volumes of these awful beverages are daily permitted on board navy ships is beyond me. I offered the drink to Mad Niko and Mild-mannered Niko. Both of them were from Greece. It is most strange that this frigate of the Royal Navy is manned by almost as many foreigners as sons of England. Working, sleeping and eating together in messes and watches up and down the *Boneta* were men from every part of the globe. Africans, Asians, Scandinavians, black and white men from the West Indies, and even a couple of men from France. My mess is where some of the landmen and least able seamen are quartered. On this ship we are the lowest of the low.

'You've made a lot of men very happy and rich, Black Prince,' joked one of my messmates. 'We all wagered you'd stay up on that mast as long as you had to, we knew you weren't no coward, didn't we, lads?' Not every voice in the mess answered, 'Aye!', but enough did to satisfy my pride.

I ate my dolphin-glop then immediately lost myself to sleep once more. I was rudely shocked to wakefulness by cries of 'Granny!', 'Gran-Gran!', 'Ahoy, Granny-man!', 'Ho there, Granny-boy!', 'Granny Gran-Gran!', 'Granny Williams, avast there!', 'Hey, me Granny!', 'Granny Williams!'. I tried to bury my head under the light sheet of canvas that served as a blanket because the approaching 'Granny' of popular acclaim was none other than my own brother, Able Seaman Patrick Williams. Patrick has served at sea before and is in every respect an excellent, if not the best able seaman currently manning the rigging of the *Boneta*. He is the epitome of manliness and in all aspects, save one, is he the model of an alert, steadfast and dutiful mariner – he is a Williams, after all.

My brother's only failing is his mortal terror of rats. He cannot abide them in any way, shape or form whatsoever; not their coiled, semi-reptilian tails, not their gluey, grimy fur, not their razor-sharp teeth, not their shuttling, bobbing, sideboard-skating, scuttling, fidgety, gristly, rotten, pooey, subterranean, herky-jerky supreme nastiness. No. He did not like them. Yet if the *Boneta* belonged to any it was to the rats that dwelled amongst us in such supernatural abundance. This was *their* territory. My dear brother, a hero of the mizzen mast, was known for being unable to sleep in his hammock unless he was wrapped from head to foot in several layers of different materials. His behaviour was far from irrational. I had been brought out of slumber on occasion by a nibble or scamper from our rodent shipmates. I did not mind them. Patrick did. It was embarrassing. I looked in on him once during our first few days at sea and found him asleep, bound from head to foot like an insect's larva. His head was multibly tied in scarves of all fabrics and designs. He even took to wearing the scarves during the daytime for fear of rat droppings tumbling from the ceiling or the upper rigging on to his head as he went about his business. Again, this was not irrational, but it earned him the name of 'Granny Williams'. He has been known to scream in a most umanly manner upon the sight of one dancing on his bare foot, say, or to see another sitting up on its haunches as it bids him a ratty good morning from his hammock pillow. This behaviour is not only embarrassing, I also find it strange. As a child in Freetown, he often led me on lengthy expeditions up into the mountains and along rivers. To my young eyes he seemed the master of every environment. The most vicious beasts of the forest and plain seemed to disturb him not a whit. Wild pigs, snakes, big cats and crocodiles were of no consequence to Patrick Williams. My admiration for him would have been greatly diminished had I heard the baby-squeal he emitted when confronted by a solitary rat.

'Look lively there, landman!' Patrick kicked me gently. 'How are you feeling?'

51

'God be with you, Patrick. I am well, thank you very much.' I raised myself to face him. I believe Patrick and I have spoken man to man probably fewer than six times since the *Boneta* left England. I always felt as if I danced on the edge of his contempt. My brother has always been slow to forgive my mistakes and I had no wish to reignite his bad feelings for me.

'Well done, Jupiter. You showed that Hines boy a thing or two about our Williams fortitude!'

'I think he knows well our family strength, Patrick. What he seeks is our utmost obedience.'

I tried to take my brother in with a glance. He presented a truly comic figure in his old woman's shawl-like tartan headscarf. Since joining the crew he has adopted a number of wholly artificial and irritating seafaring ways. His walk is now bow-legged. A plug of chewing tobacco is permanently wedged in his cheek. He affects the ridiculous talk of the navy: *me hearty, me bucko, me bucko-mate, arrr, avast, belay*, and so on in an accent that he imagines inclines the listener to believe he hails from Devon or Cornwall. Which is not to say that there are not black men from these places (indeed, prior to boarding the *Boneta* I would have sworn on the Bible that could never be the case), but my brother is definitely not one of them. He is an African. Today, he even carried a lidded pewter tankard like a proper old drunken sailor. I found myself laughing inside and wondering why he had come to see me.

For a while we said nothing. Just as the silence was about to become uncomfortable, my brother in the tartan scarf said, 'Jupiter, you do remember we have a brother still in London, don't you?'

'Ah, little Robert, of course, yes.'

For a moment I beheld our gifted younger sibling in my mind's eye. Brilliant Robert with his eyes for ever fixed on to the script of some political or scientific gazette. Poor Robert, whom we had left behind in London in the service of a gang of Wapping wastrels. Brave Robert, who had risked all to save me and was now paying the price. How could I have forgotten him?

'Today is his birthday. He is now fourteen years old.'

'Oh.'

I had forgotten all of this, of course. I never remember birthdays. My own passed last week and I would have forgotten that as well had it not been for Patrick coming to wish me well.

Patrick lifted the lid of the tankard and the unholy stench of navy rum assailed my nostrils. 'We will drink,' he proclaimed firmly. 'Drink to the memory of our brother, Robert Williams. Then let us drink to our family. To the honour of the Williams'.'

Patrick tipped the tankard and gulped twice. He passed it to me. I have never developed a taste for any kind of brewed beverage. Wine, beer, gin, rum, brandy, none have held the slightest attraction for me. Patrick had been of a similar mind for as long as I could remember. Given that our father had been a minister, amongst other things, I was all the more shocked to see the ease and pleasure with which Patrick dispatched the drink. For the sake of ceremony I swallowed the nastiness and managed not to be sick.

'You drank but once, Jupiter. You must swallow twice. Once for Robert and once more for the family. Drink again.'

I took a second swig and as I did so I tried my utmost, through my disgust, to be true to the ritual. I summoned memories of our family home in Freetown. I invoked the words of my father to me as we left for England: *You must never let the white man beat you.* I recalled father addressing meetings with Mr Kizell and Mr Gooding under the big cotton tree. I remembered father's many businesses and his missions to the tribes inland who had no knowledge of Christ or the Gospels. Yes, we had much to be proud of and the memory brought me to the brink of tears, and it was strange how much easier it was to remember now that I was half drunk.

I even conjured a vague image of our mother who had died giving birth to little Robert. Or not-so-little Robert. Fourteen. What mischief was he up to now?

Patrick bent towards me in a conspiratorial manner. 'This ship has been tasked with attacking the pirate fleet in Morocco,' he whispered. 'There is talk amongst the marines of a strange new craft in the hold.'

'Oh, that must be the beardy-man, stinky cheese poo-ship, if my nose is any guide,' I quipped.

'What was that, Jupiter?'

'Oh, nothing, Patrick. I was jesting. But it does smell foully down there. What else have you heard? What do you mean, a new ship? Is it like a cutter, a new launch or yawl?'

'No, Jupiter. None of those ships. Truth to tell I do not know, at least I can't make sense of what they say. Whatever they are doing is not our concern. All I know is that soon we will be on African soil once again.'

'African? You mean Moroccan soil, surely?'

'You are the one with the expensive education, Jupiter. Tell me, on which continent will you find Morocco?'

'But those people are followers of Mohammed. They are the most atrocious enslavers of our people.'

Patrick stared dully at me. 'Remind me, where exactly have we just come from and under whose flag do we now sail? Yes, Great Britain, queen of slavers all. In England our people are all slaves, servants, sailors or soldiers. We can die or dig for them. Nothing else.'

Before I could beg to differ based on the benefit of my personal experience of black life in London, Patrick continued, 'In the Arab lands, yes we do slave, truth to tell, but our people also occupy some of the very highest positions from Turkey to Tangiers.'

'You mean they are Mohammedans.'

'And what of it?'

'What of it? They are Mohammedans! They worship a false god!'

'Oh yes, they are unbelievers, aren't they? That means they will be tortured eternally on a lake of fire when they die, doesn't it?'

'Of course! As will you if you do not accept the son of God as your Lord and saviour. You know this well enough. Why do you mock both me and the one true faith?'

Patrick brushed my concerns aside and pulled his stool closer to me. He whispered, 'How did you like the cheese, Jupiter?'

'You know I hate cheese, Patrick, but thank you all the same.'

'You didn't look at it then?'

'No, I cast it overboard.'

'You did *what*?'

'I threw it away. It would have made me vomit.'

'I did not expect you to eat it. I had hidden something inside the cheese to raise your spirits.'

I had no idea what he was talking about.

'A map!' he hissed. 'There was a tiny map I drew showing where our position should be when we arrive off the African coast. On the back were instructions detailing our escape.'

Our escape?

'If what I'm hearing is true, I reckon we'll be able to get a small boat over the side and be away towards the coast in very little time.'

'So, Patrick, you didn't think to ask me before including me in your plans?' He shook his head. 'It is our duty to return to Sierra Leone as soon as possible. We must re-establish the family business and reclaim our property as soon as possible. Our country needs leadership. We must go home any way we can.'

I knew that everything he said was true but, despite the harshness of naval life, I did not want to escape. I actually liked being at sea.

'And how are we to get from Morocco to Sierra Leone? By camel?'

'Do not mock me, boy!' In that instant, Patrick looked and sounded exactly like our father.

[*6*]

'Ah, reading again, Black Prince?' the surgeon asked. 'A medical book again?'

I closed the copy of *Northcote's Marine Practice* that I'd been flicking through. I have access to no other reading on the *Boneta* except the Bible and Father had already seen to it that we were familiar with that book in its entirety before we left Sierra Leone on our travels. Without Druce's medical texts I would go mad with boredom. Besides, they interest me. The locations and relationship of the various muscles, bones, veins and nerves in the human body are intriguing to me.

However, on a ship like this it is preferable to be caught with a loaded pistol or a knife against another's throat than with a printed matter of any kind, and I believe Dr Druce is fascinated by the idea of a literate black person.

There was very little work to be done that afternoon. The only patient to present himself was a seaman who had slipped and cut his leg on a rusty nail. I helped Dr Druce to clean the wound before packing it with maggots and sewing it back up.

I returned to my reading.

'Ooh, that looks like a nasty bump.' The doctor pointed to my head. 'Let me take a look at it.'

He prodded. I winced.

'How did you come by this?'

'I fell, Dr Druce. There is so little room on this ship.'

'I understand. You mean you fell by the wrath of Sergeant Mills. The man is a brute.'

'He is one who hates all black people. I cannot understand it.'

The doctor slopped strong-smelling mentholated gunk on my lump and bound it with a strip of clean cloth.

'Mills is a man more to be pitied than feared. I could tell you a terrible tale of his experiences in Jamaica.'

'That is of no interest to me, I'm afraid, doctor. The thought of him in any part of the world where my people reside is too much to bear.'

'But he suffered greatly there.'

'A-good!'

'He was held prisoner by the Maroon rebels of Trelawny.'

Some of the leading families in Freetown are Maroons. As you would expect of runaway slaves who kept the British at bay for over one hundred years, they are fearsome fighters. I said: *gooood*.

'Whilst being held prisoner by them he was flogged daily until finally he was subjected to an ordeal that no man should be forced to endure. That he survived is a testament to his fortitude—'

'And to the mercy of the Maroons surely, who should have killed him had they any sense.'

'Sergeant Mills was half the man he used to be, Jupiter. Do you understand?'

I swallowed. I understood perfectly. And while I would not wish his torment on anyone (not even him), I will always regret that the black rebels had not cut his tongue out instead.

'And so you see, you can't blame him, really, can you?' Druce enquired. But I can and I do. How many of our people are tortured and beaten, yet do we treat all whites as if each and every one of them is an irredeemable monster? That such a rancorous set of rogues should rule so much of the earth is a thing beyond my understanding and threatens to make a nonsense of all true religion. 'And which section are you reading now, boy?'

'I am looking at ligatures, doctor.'

'Ah, ligatures, the delicate art of tying off blood

vessels!' Dr Druce clasped his hands before him, seemingly entranced by the idea. 'How would you like to perform a ligature, young man?'

'Why, sir, very much. Very much indeed.'

'How would you like to tie off a blood vessel right now?'

'But, doctor—'

'I will teach you all you need to know.'

'But how can you perform a ligature?' I declared. 'We have no patients.'

'That's where you're wrong.' He chuckled.

As I approached the manger I carefully worked a slipknot into the length of rope I was carrying behind my back. I have trapped and killed animals before, but for some reason I knew that ending Lucifer's life would not be easy. I peered at him over the gate. It was a shock to discover that goats could curl their lips and snarl. It was as if the goat had foreknowledge of his fate.

He stared me in the eye. I took a step back from the gate when I realized the animal had bitten through the rope that secured him to the wall. He lowered his head, snarled more deeply and charged. I didn't know that goats could jump. Skip, yes. Frolic and gambol, certainly. But to behold a fully grown goat practically levitate to waist height and sail towards you over a fence is a fearsome sight indeed. I was away from Lucifer and his horns before his hooves struck the deck. My feet whisked me across the deck and up the steps to the poopdeck. The goat's hooves clattered perilously close behind me. Lucifer chased me through a gaggle of midshipmen. One of the ship's officers was screaming something I had no time to understand, whereupon all hands on deck fell to mighty gales of laughter. I vaulted over the poopdeck rail to the main deck, but Lucifer was too fast. He merely *skidded* down the stairs and joined me in an instant. He lowered his terrible horns and charged again. I ran around the crane above the hold hoping to make it to one of the gangways below decks, but the animal was to quick for me and seemed to anticipate my every move. Besides, my audience was growing. Sailors, drawn to the main deck by the commotion, cheerfully blocked every point of escape and hunkered down to see how the episode would conclude. Each charge from the goat and every dodge on my part drew waves of applause from my shipmates. As I cleared a heap of coiled ropes I landed badly and fell. The impact of Lucifer's horns in my lower back was not as sharp as I feared they might be, but there was a lot of force behind them. This blow earned the goat a massive ovation from the crew.

I rolled away and stood up. There was no way that I, Jupiter Williams, would permit myself to be gored by a mere goat before a crowd of chortling buffoons. I had no jacket to throw over him and would have to use my bare hands and feet. It was going to be ugly.

I charged at him and made a grab for his horns. He caught me once in the thigh, but I managed to hold on for a short while as he bucked and swerved. Lucifer was incredibly strong and I was thrown about the dwindling space on the deck like a toy. Before I knew it he had twisted the horns out of my grip altogether and butted me directly in my stomach. I lost my balance and fell to the deck in great pain, unable to breathe. I could not stand. The goat trotted off to the ship's starboard rail then turned *to get a better run at me*! This could not be how my life would end, amidst the awful sound of those hooves and the callow laughter of bored seamen. What shame, what shame! I shut my eyes and curled into as tight a ball as I could. I heard Lucifer's snorting, I heard the whoops from the rigging, and I heard *thdoub*! Then silence.

I opened my eyes to see Lucifer motionless, standing barely inches from where I lay. He blinked at the hands on deck, who were also quiet, then at those in the rigging, who were just as still.

Thdoub!

I saw a small lead weight bounce off the animal's skull. His legs buckled as he collapsed in a heap beside me.

My name was being called from one of the masts. It was Patrick, my brother. He saluted me and brandished his slingshot with the broadest smile I'd seen on his face in a very long while.

'Why, the beast is perfectly stunned. How so?' Dr Druce tipped Lucifer's head this way and that.

'He was struck by a lead weight from a slingshot, sir.'

'Quite amazing!' The doctor unrolled a set of surgical instruments. He extracted a tiny knife and a pair of forceps then handed them to me with great ceremony.

'If you will be so good as to make the first incision, Jupiter . . .'

'You want me to cut it *now*? But the goat is still alive.'

'Barely alive, boy. He is but a few heartbeats away from eternity before he will be butchered for the captain's table.'

Hesitantly, I made a broad cut across the set of

leg muscles Dr Druce indicated, then another from the centre of that upwards. Using forceps I prised the skin apart.

Dr Druce probed through the cut, pulled up a blood vessel and cut it. He passed me an oddly shaped needle.

'Work it gently under the artery now. Try to make your movements firm yet smooth, Jupiter. Right, you've got the artery clear now. Time to tie it off and stop the flow of blood.'

The doctor dangled a barely visible thread in front of me. 'This is what you will tie off with. It's the finest silk. Very expensive, but normally it separates after fifteen days and all is well.' He passed it to me.

'Twist each end around the second finger of each hand. That's right, give yourself a little slack now. Then slide each index finger along the ligature. You're nearly there, Jupiter. Finally, thrust out with each so as to close the knot.'

I looked down at what I had done. The artery had been perfectly closed up. The seal was immaculate, not a drop of blood anywhere. Dr Druce's mouth was open in astonishment.

Francis knocked and stepped through the door in a single movement. He was carrying an enormous carving knife. 'Is he dead yet, Dr Druce? The cook says he can't wait, needs to get it seasoned soonish!'

'Go away, child!' snapped the doctor. 'Five more minutes.'

Francis shrugged and left us in contemplation of my ligature.

'Jupiter Williams, that really is not a bad piece of work. Not bad at all. You may have the makings of a decent sawbones. Who knows?'

[7]

We stood with Oyster Loycher and Midshipman Hines at the prow of the *Boneta*. Eight of us, all new hands, looked out to sea staring at the long beam of the bowsprit as it loomed over it and dipped into the waters from time to time.

'Right, now you must always endeavour to maintain your position as you proceed to pass nine or eleven turns of the rope over the bowsprit,' said the young gentleman.

Nine or eleven? Why not simply say ten? Why did everything in the Royal Navy have to be so complicated? Mild-mannered Niko was the unfortunate sailor drafted in to demonstrate this new technique. He climbed skilfully along the beam and, as if climbing up a rope, pulled himself along until he was at the tip of the bowsprit.

The bosun appeared pleased with the new crewman's progress.

'You see, the landman has completed this task without too much trouble and is now holding steady.

In order to complete the task, he will require the assistance of a more experienced hand.'

We all breathed a sigh of relief. I, for one, did not fancy my chances on that dipping, bucking pole above the sea. Oyster Loycher's scanned the decks and rigging. He pointed skywards. 'Them lads there, Mr Hines. One of them'll do nicely. Strong lads all.'

The midshipman looked up at a group of sailors coming down the rigging from the topmasts. 'Very well, bosun.' He nodded. 'Pick your man.'

'Now one of these topmen here will join you along the 'sprit to help you with your round turns and your clinches fast against the cleats,' Oyster Loycher informed Niko, who was only just managing to maintain his position on the bowsprit.

'You there, topman. *Black* topman!' Oyster Loycher had singled Patrick out of a line of sailors sloping away from their watch to a long-awaited break.

'Shift yourself up with him and have a care that his turns are crossed forward, hove tight and well nippered.'

I didn't have the faintest idea what he was talking about, but I'm sure there was a more straightforward way of saying it.

'Aye, bosun!' said Patrick sullenly as he spat out,

then pocketed a plug of tobacco.

With swift, expert movements Patrick shinned his way along the bowsprit and joined Niko.

'You'll be a-gammoning now. Let's see it. Sharply!'

Oyster Loycher threw a length of rope that was attached to a foresail to Patrick. I had never seen Patrick at work before. I was impressed. He was a living demonstration of the cliché that 'good sailors are born not made'. He caught the line thrown by the bosun in a very deft fashion then flicked it against the underside of the bowsprit like a whiplash so that it would half wind itself about the bowsprit at Niko's end. He motioned for Niko to secure the rope by winding it fast through several turns at the tip. Niko was clutching the very end of the bowsprit. He was facing us, that is to say he was facing us occasionally because the ship was now bucking wildly and plunging its prow into the sea every second or third dip, taking Niko through the surging waters as it went. He was thoroughly drenched and seemed to shiver uncontrollably. I believe he was shocked out of his mind. For no better apparent reason than to exercise his seniority, Sergeant Mills grabbed the bosun's speaking trumpet and hollered, 'You there, blackie, lay fast to the landman immediately and take him through the windings.' Patrick, whose back was to those of us on deck, turned to question the reasoning behind this order. Sergeant Mills positioned himself so that he could attack my brother with the knout if he decided to leave the bowsprit. My brother barely had a secure hold on it himself. Patrick looked to Midshipman Hines and Oyster Loycher in desperation.

'Lay fast to him and wind on, able seaman!' intoned the midshipman reluctantly.

The lowest of murmurs ran through the men. Patrick eventually said, 'Aye, aye, Mr Hines,' and started to pull himself towards Niko. Soon Patrick and Niko were face to face at the uttermost tip of the bucking ship as they disappeared and reappeared from the ocean. Patrick had managed to get a grip on Niko's belt and was doing his best to pull the Greek sailor into a safer position. Down they went again, and up they came, coughing and choking.

'Wind on now, both of you!' ordered Sergeant Mills.

'He means to murder 'em,' whispered someone behind me.

'Begging your pardon, Sergeant Mills,' shouted Midshipman Hines, 'but those men must return to the deck. These are no waters for gammoning.' He turned to Oyster Loycher. 'Bosun, command those two men to dismount from the bowsprit immediately.' Oyster Loycher was about to comply when a stream of gargled Greek drew our eyes back to the bowsprit. Patrick and Niko were about to plough through a new wave. My brother was trying to calm the other sailor, who seemed very close to losing his grip on the ship altogether. Niko was babbling something that I'm sure was nonsense even in Greek. The bowsprit went down once more. It resurfaced with only one sailor clinging to it.

No one said a word as Patrick inched backwards off the bowsprit. Sergeant Mills blew once on his whistle and two marines came trotting to the prow. 'I want you to put this black man in irons!' he squealed.

'On what charge, sergeant?' asked the midshipman.

'Why, insubordination, Mr Hines . . . and murder! You were a witness to it. So was the bosun and all these men here. You told the darkie, I mean the able seaman, to move along the bowsprit and hold on to his shipmate, did you not?' Mills spoke directly to the bosun, though his comments were directed at Mr Hines.

It took all my self-control (and the restraining arms of four other seamen) not to launch myself at Mills. Patrick was back on deck coughing wretchedly. He glowered at the marine with open hatred and Mills's face glowed with delight at the approaching triumph of his powers. He knew there would be a flogging tomorrow morning.

[8]

At first light the next morning the order rang around the *Boneta*: 'All hands witness punishment, ahoy!'

This command produced a dismal sensation amongst the crew. We mustered as best we could on the crane-crowded deck. I pushed my way to the front rank, determined to have the best view of all the actors in the scene about to unfold.

The officers, in full dress uniform, stood to the left side. I spotted Sergeant Mills smirking amongst the ship's company of marines lined up behind them. He seemed to be bobbing on the balls of his feet with excitement. I made sure he registered my stare and, as I did so, I drew comfort from the sensation of the slingshot and the small lead weights I had stuffed down my shirt.

There was no sign whatsoever of Midshipman Hines.

None of us aboard the *Boneta* (especially those who were pressed into service) expected fairness from naval regulations, but the dark and absolute humiliation that Patrick was about to undergo moved all but the most hardened sailors to thoughts of mutiny. Niko had been a universally popular fellow who had died unnecessarily. He would be missed. And, for all the mockery my brother endured, he was a very valuable seaman whose absence from the mizzen mast would cause no end of problems.

'Bosun, the prisoner, if you please,' Captain Hibbert ordered.

Oyster Loycher and four of his mates escorted Patrick up from the brig towards a section of grating where Dr Druce waited. The sound of Patrick's chains was dreadful. We removed our hats. On a nod from the captain, Patrick's shirt was removed and he was tied to the grating.

A gasp ran through the crew as my brother's back was revealed. A mass of cross-hatched welts had been etched into his flesh from a flogging he'd received when enslaved some years previously. It was clear that three lashes would break the skin into a bloody pulp. The pain from six lashes would render him unconscious. Twelve would surely kill him.

The charge was read out and the sentence declared: *seventy-two lashes*.

Behind me an older sailor muttered under his

breath, 'The king has seen it in his mercy to set an upper limit of one thousand lashes for his boys in the navy, gawdblessim. It's only fair, don't you think, Black Prince?' At the risk of incurring punishment myself for breaking ranks, I turned to stare into his face. He was serious. His sympathy was genuine.

The bosun's mates would take turns to flog him. Twelve lashes per mate. They drew lots for their turns. Baby Brookes would be the first to lay on.

The bosun's mate was no stranger to administering floggings, but he was hugely subdued and lacking in vigour as he opened the green baize bag and shook out a nine-stranded knotted whip known as the cat-o'-nine-tails. Baby cracked the cat loudly, glaring at Sergeant Mills as he did so. He cast a succession of glances around the assembled seamen. His look of suppressed indignation acknowledged me in passing. It was only then I realized that he was not looking at the whole crew, but only at the other black crewmen.

There must have been more than twenty men and boys of African origin on the *Boneta*. Our backgrounds varied. Some were born within the sound of Bow Bells, others hailed from Barbados, Baltimore or Africa's Bullom Shore. Some (including Patrick) had spent part of their lives as other people's property. We were of all ranks from cabin boy to midshipman, yet for every one of us a flogging was an act of the ultimate degradation.

I did not even know the names of all the other black men on the ship. It had never occurred to me to befriend every one of them simply on account of their colour. But now, we were all one, united in common feeling. For black seamen there was no such thing as an *ordinary* flogging. Every instance of corporal punishment against non-white seamen, no matter how well deserved and regardless of the charge, brought us all back instantly to that greater world of slave factories and plantations where all dignity and joy could be extinguished at the end of a white man's whip. Today it was made all the worse by having the punishment initially administered by Baby Brookes, a black seaman. The bosun's mate's eyes sought our forgiveness and promised revenge at the same time.

Whereas only hours before the *Boneta*'s crew had eaten, slept, drank and worked together as one, we stood now as two different sets of people observing two entirely different events. Black and White.

And where was the ship's highest-ranking black seaman? The right words at the right time from Edward Hines could have prevented this punishment from taking place. I scanned the assembled crew, but he was nowhere to be seen. It was probably just as well for him as he certainly would probably have been a third target for my slingshot.

'Do your duty, bonun's mate,' bellowed the captain. 'Lay on with a will and don't favour the man, or you shall take his place!'

A drum roll commenced. Baby Brookes flexed the whip to its full length and swung it towards Patrick. We all heard Patrick gasp in a most explosive manner. I could see he was using all his strength to stop himself writhing in agony, and I looked away, recalling our father's words: *Never let the white man beat you!*

'One!' cried Oyster Loycher.

My right hand snuck under my shirt. I hefted the two lead weights and shuffled them into the slingshot for a double strike.

Baby Brookes delivered a second lash. The scarred skin broke in places. Blood began to flow.

'Two!'

The slingshot was now loose in my hand, and with the crew's attention fixed firmly on the flogging, I took a sidestep and readied the weapon to target Sergeant Mills.

'*Sail ho!*'

Captain Hibbert's rapidly raised hand brought the

deck to a standstill. We followed his gaze all the way up to the topmast.

'*Sail ho!*' It was Midshipman Hines, calling from the ship's highest point.

Captain Hibbert motioned for a further pause. 'Masthead there, lad?'

'Aye, sir.'

'What does she look like?'

'A French frigate, sir, standing towards us. Nay, bearing down upon us.'

'How do they bear, Mr Hines? Do they seem athwart our hawse at all?'

The midshipman replied with a stream of naval gibberish which included the words: 'two and a half points', 'lee-bow', 'rising fast' and 'being abreast'. All of which I translated as meaning a French ship would be upon us within twenty minutes.

'Belay that punishment, bosun! All hands clear the ship for action, ahoy! Beat to quarters, if you please, and show our colours!' called Captain Hibbert.

The ship came alive as if one being. Deck officers scrambled for telescopes. Ranks broke and men scattered to their duties at all points of the vessel. The men had not been in any mood to witness punishment, and they rushed keenly to their battle stations. It was as if they sought to burn off the shame of Patrick's flogging in the heat of battle.

I dawdled on deck long enough to see my brother being untied from the grating by Dr Druce and a very apologetic-looking Baby Brookes. Patrick hurried away to his battle station at one of the twenty-four-pounder guns.

I had never seen the crew so animated. Even little Francis was caught up in the mood of the moment. His face was a picture of malicious glee. He was at his battle station behind a row of eight-pounders where he crouched with his canister, ready to fetch and carry gunpowder as it was needed. Like the rest of the gun crew, Francis had stripped to the waist and wore a large knotted handkerchief around his head. He waved at me and pointed out to sea where a frigate-sized ship was blurring into view. The *Boneta* could certainly hold its own against almost any ship. She carried twenty-four twenty-four-pounders on her main deck and fourteen eight-pounders on her quarterdeck.

'Frenchies!' he hollered as if he was about to play skittles. He punched the air and I swear he growled, 'Arr-arrrr!'

I wished I could have remained on deck and played a more active role in the battle, but my station was below decks with the surgeon. With a heavy heart I made my way to the galley where I collected one pail of boiling water and one of cold from the cook. I carried them to the wardroom, carefully angling them away from the press of charging bodies in the narrow walkways. By the time Dr Druce appeared, I had already neatly laid out his larger saws and scalpels together with wads of gauze and strips of clean cotton. A small fire was reddening up tools in a brazier. A roll of mouldy canvas had been thrown over the table where he would perform his operations. I had covered the floor with a thick layer of sawdust.

Wordlessly, the surgeon laid out his drugs, his personal set of small knives, clamps and needles, a bottle of overproof rum and a Bible.

'This is your first time under fire, I take it, Jupiter?'

'Indeed not, sir,' I declared, recalling my narrow escapes from death by pistol in London.

'No, I mean under fire from cannons. At sea.'

'It is, sir.'

'Do you have a very strong stomach, boy? Does the sight of much blood appal you or induce faintness of mind?'

I glared at him as if he was exceptionally rude and stupid.

'You are about to behold scenes that no man should see.' He rested a hand on my shoulder and peered into my face. 'You are a stalwart fellow and I can see that you are impatient for the fight to begin. I can also see that you feel your place is above decks, manning the guns perhaps, or positioned up in the rigging with a musket or smoke bomb in your fist. But there is more than enough work to be done down here, and glory. I will need you to stand ready and stand steady whatever occurs this day, regardless of . . . This is by far the worst place to be on a frigate in the heat of battle.'

I doubted this greatly. Surely the very worst place would be on deck amidst the all fire and fury where you had every chance of witnessing the effects of cannon balls punching through your shipmates. But I nodded dutifully as if I believed what he was telling me.

The structure of the *Boneta* shuddered terribly and I clutched at an edge of the table in panic. 'Have no fear. That's just the rumble of our guns being run out all together.'

The guns, now loaded, were run back in. Apart from the orders being barked from the officers' speaking-trumpets the ship fell suddenly still.

'Hark!' Dr Druce pointed to the ceiling. 'It is about to begin. We'll have tacked alongside them by now.'

The roar of the starboard guns firing all at once nearly deafened me. I dread to think what it must have done the crew manning them. I felt the *Boneta* roll away from the blast.

'Aye. They'll be feeling the full force of Brittania's broadside now! Magnificent sound!'

Moments later the sides of the ship above and below us shook under the impact of several cannon balls cracking oak. It sounded like a giant bully rapidly beating down a door with his fists.

'Hmmn, the hulls been breached, the enemy must be firing thirty-six-pounders. Fearsome things. I can't say I like the sound of that at all. Oh no.'

We had been hit!

It occurred to me that the *Boneta* might have been hulled severely, possibly below the waterline. If the ship started taking in water I would surely perish, being so far below decks. I moved to place my hands on the Holy Bible. Under my breath, I began to commend my soul to God.

'Save your prayers, my lad. We'll soon be tending to those who truly need them!'

Above the trampling footfall and screamed oaths came an almighty cracking sound followed by a creak like Hell's rusty gates being pulled open.

'My God. Chain shot aplenty. They must have struck a mast! Let us pray it is not the main. Uurgh! Bodies fallen to the deck now. Three or four. Hear that sound, boy?'

There are sounds one has never heard that are yet immediately identifiable. An unprotected human body landing on a wooden surface from a height of over one hundred feet is one of them.

'More now. Dropping from the mast tops. Say what you will about the Frenchmen, they are *superb* snipers, mores the—'

The shot that entered our wardroom must have travelled through the hull and somehow been deflected downwards on its journey from the gundeck. Its noise was not even that loud, but the missile managed to hole walls on its way in and out of the room. It came close enough to make our insides churn and rumble like they were in the grip of sharp short fever. The surgeon and I were flung into opposing corners as, miraculously, it passed between our heads and destroyed another wall on its way out to damage somewhere else.

I blasphemed.

'The ship is in much worse condition than we thought, isn't it?' I asked in absolute seriousness and mortal terror. 'That was close. Very close.' I swallowed dryly. 'What sort of shot was it, Dr Druce? Doctor?'

'Rod shot.' He sighed loudly. 'This is very bad. That was most definitely rod shot, yes. Dreadful stuff. Oh Lord! Lord, help me.' He turned around very slowly with his hands out before him. 'Jupiter?' The surgeon blinked. The surgeon blinked blood. He fingered his face and moaned like a cow being crudely slaughtered. I shuddered to see that his eyes and eyelids were feathered with the finest splinters. Thirty of them, perhaps: thirty thin stalks of the most extreme wooden pain. Though he must have been in the direst agony, Druce did not so much as grunt as he felt his way to the table. He managed to lay down and remain still.

'Jupiter, the tweezers! Fast boy, fast!' he rasped.

I steeled my heart and lowered myself over the man's quivering face to set about removing the splinters one by one with as much speed and precision as I could summon. By the time I had finished I was holding back my own tears. Though the doctor had not shed a single tear himself, a smell in the room indicated that he had voided his bowels during my operation. I squeezed out some chamomile cloths and bound them around his bleeding eyes.

'God bless you, Jupiter. God bless you. Now to the others. Look to the others. I will direct you.'

In my concern for Dr Druce, I had ignored the growing number of wounded men being laid out behind me in the wardroom and yet more dumped behind them in the corridor almost as far as the stairs of the hatchway.

The first casualty was the master-at-arms, Mr Foxton. He was by no means the first in the 'queue' but he was the senior seaman in the pile at my heels and the one with the loudest voice. His trousers below the knee were black with blood. I hauled him on to the table and cut away at the cloth. I wish I hadn't. A fractured bone poked through ripped skin and muscle. I hurriedly described what I was facing to Dr Druce.

'You must immediately sever that limb above the broken bone!'

Before I could protest he had felt his way to an open store box. He threw a screw-tourniquet in my direction.

'I know we can rely on our Black Prince. I've seen you reading and you've a sure hand. Apply this to Mr

Foxton where required, Jupiter. Tightly now.' I fastened the little nest of leather straps around the master's upper leg, some way above the wound. The master screamed. I had to concentrate: had to try to remember precisely how the tourniquet was going to save Foxton's life. He was making too much noise. I couldn't think, so I rammed a gag down his mouth in a most brutal fashion. Turning back to the attached tourniquet, I wound the screw as far as it could go in an effort to stop the flow of blood.

'Have you done, lad? Is it tight and good?' Druce enquired. He was already kicking a box of amputation instruments towards me.

'The bone saw! The bone saw. You must use it!' He uttered those words like a priest administering the last rites.

I hefted the smaller bone saw and looked from it to Mr Foxton's destroyed leg and back again, trying to estimate its efficiency. Could my total inexperience really worsen his distress? It seemed very unlikely. I started sawing with a will through the break already in the bone. I worked away heartily, not really knowing what I was doing when suddenly I was seized by the idea of saving as much of the leg as possible. To this end I sliced diagonally downwards through the muscle to determine the best cut. The floor was soon slick with blood. Halfway through the leg I paused to swap blades: I'd need a finger saw for the finer work through the surrounding ligaments.

Mr Foxton managed to cough the gag from his mouth. He pulled his pistol and cocked it against my head. 'You'll cut quick and cut clean now, you black bastard, or I'll blow your fuzzy head clean off your shoulders! Cut, man! Cut and use the big'un!' He motioned towards the larger saw. So I cut on until what was left of the leg below the knee dropped to the deck.

'You're a good lad, Jupiter! A good lad.' Foxton made safe his firearm and slumped back on to the table. I envied both his and the doctor's ability to be silent while suffering greatly. I knew that would be beyond me, though I must add that the master's howls as I applied a red-hot iron to seal his wound before binding were loud enough to drown out the noise of the battle raging above.

My next patient was a marine sniper who had been caught in the back by grape shot. While reflecting on the irony of a sniper being shot in the back, I managed to cut off the burned clothing. Because the grape shot had welded to his skin in places I had to remove the pellets in his flesh by jabbing at them with an aneurysm needle as I'd misplaced the tweezers after messing with Dr Druce's eyes. The marine shot off the table in agony. I held him face down on the messy floor and hacked at his back while he writhed like an eel. I picked away the bits of filthy shirt that the shot had driven into his body then cleaned the wounds with vinegar to avoid infection. I ordered the patient away as it was clear that even if bent double he could still carry himself.

After him there was a blurred, desolate eternity of filleting, stitching, poking, gagging, mopping, mummying, slicing, folding, sweating, bone-chipping, slapping, hair-singeing, scalp-scraping, gouging, sawing, skin-stretching and bad language.

I remember slopping some poor wretches intestines back inside his stomach before sewing it up. I was never a clever stitcher, but I am proud, not to say amazed, that my needlework stood me in good stead throughout that day.

'Young gentleman coming through! Young gentleman coming through!' came a cry from the corridor. Mr Hines was delivered shoulder-high on to the filthy table. Blood spurted wildly from a vessel somewhere between his shoulder and neck. He was coughing blood and breathing blood.

Immediately I whipped a substantial length of bandage from a basket and wound it about the midshipman's neck. It was to no avail. As I wound the cloth it seemed to act like a magnet, drawing blood in even greater surges from his body.

'Dr Druce,' I called, unable to mask the helplessness in my voice. 'I don't know what to do. It's his neck. It's bleeding.'

'Who is your patient, Jupiter?'

'Who is my patient! With all possible respect, sir, the patient's name is of no—'

'Jupiter!' He called my name as if bringing a dog to heel. 'What is his name?'

'It's Mr Hines, doctor. The midshipman.'

'Oh dear. Oh dear . . . I see, then this really is a matter of the greatest importance. Listen to me most carefully and do exactly as I say.'

'Yes, sir.'

'The first thing is to staunch the flow of blood from his neck.'

'It's already bandaged, sir. It's no good. He's bleeding all over the place.'

'Can he breathe?'

'Badly, sir. He is spraying blood.'

'Good Lord! Jupiter, you must cut into his neck, isolate the blood vessel, tie it closed and cut once more to enable the boy to breathe through his lower throat.'

I had no idea what he was talking about, but it sounded like an atrocious procedure, and one that I was singularly unfit to perform. But I found myself declaring in a voice which grew from soft to firm: 'I will do my best, sir. Guide me through it, if you please.'

My initial cuts into the young officer's neck were made difficult by the fact that he was holding my wrists in an improbably powerful grip for one so afflicted. I managed to nick his skin deeply rather than advance under it. As I felt his strength fading, I wrenched myself from his grasp and tried to cut again. This time I cut well and cut deeply. Too deeply perhaps. Blood now flowed from every point along the new incision. My hands were slippery with the stuff and I could no longer hold the knife firmly.

'What do I do now, Dr Druce?' I wailed.

'Do what I told you. Is the blood vessel a large one? Is it an artery?'

'I think so,' I said. In truth, I had no real idea if it was a vein or an artery, apart from a notion that volume of blood it spouted indicated it might be the latter.

'Tie it off immediately, like I showed you. Remember how we did it with the goat?'

I struggled to remember anything. Hines's face was turning grey. Bubbled blood appeared at his nostrils. I plunged my bare hands into his open neck to feel out the blood vessel.

'I have it, sir. I have it.' The end of the blood vessel was pinched between the fingertips of my right hand.

'Well done, lad. Now tie off and make haste. Remember, press down with the thumb and pull up from underneath with the artery forceps. You can do it.'

I thumbed the artery firmly against a flap of skin and reached for the forceps. As I brought them to his neck, the young gentleman coughed a fine mist of blood all over me. I wiped the mess from my eyes with both sleeves then looked down. The artery had vanished. It had been whipped back down into his body as if on a spring.

'How goes the tying off, Jupiter?'

'It's gone, sir. I've lost it. I can't find it. It's gone!'

Midshipman Hines sat upright in a single motion as if suddenly possessed by some diabolical energy. He clutched at my collar. 'The captain. Call the captain, I need to see him!' he gasped.

It was all I could do to hold him and remind him

that a battle was still raging around us.

He raised his hand, and I don't know whether it was to slap or to bless me, but it was the very last thing Edward Hines did in this world.

He died breathing a cloud of blood into my face. I could do nothing to save him. Even my half-remembered, half-felt prayers had proved useless.

'You did your best, Jupiter.' Dr Druce was by my side. 'You did well.'

Yes, I believe I did do my best that day.

I did do my very best.

Didn't I?

[9]

The amount of damage the ship had sustained was unbelievable. Several crewmen had died.

We had got off lightly, by all accounts. Another ship, one of our escorts, had been sunk in the battle. The French ship had turned and run after a spirited assault.

I spent my time off duty turning in my hammock and staring into the gloom of the gundeck. All around me men whimpered softly from their wounds. Others stifled tears recollecting the loss of their fellows. The hammering and sawing of the carpenters repairing the deck and masts only served to remind me of the ghastly grind of human bone and gristle under my surgeon's saws. I had never been so tired in my life. I lacked the strength or willpower even to change my shirt, which even now, hours later, was still wet and reeking with the blood of others. I could neither sleep nor rest. Whenever I closed my eyes the screams of my patients and the vision of Dr Druce's splinter-flecked eyeballs came back to haunt me with redoubled intensity. Try as I might I found no comfort in prayer. I must have muttered every prayer and psalm I knew at least twice that night, yet none could summon the peace my soul demanded.

'Mills!' Niko hissed in my ear. 'He's on his way here.'

The words were barely out of his mouth when the marines' sergeant burst into our sleeping quarters. 'You!' he snarled, pointing at me with his knout. 'You're wanted by the captain. This instant.' The soldier looked as exhausted as I felt. Being too fatigued to swipe me with the knotted rope, he batted the air about me instead. 'Follow me.'

Niko crossed himself as I hurried behind Mills. I should have been very worried – an audience with a ship's captain is seldom a pleasant experience for a young landman, but I was so weary and beset with frightful reminiscences that even the thought of a court martial would have been but light relief. Besides, what more could befall me this day?

Sergeant Mills shoved me into the captain's cabin with such force that I almost joined the clutter on his desk.

Captain Hibbert stank of old sweat and strong drink. He stood with his back turned to me, staring out the stern window.

'You will drink with me, landman,' he commanded.

'I am obliged to thank you for your offer, captain, but navy rum is not to my ta—'

A blow from Mills's knotted rope to my skull reminded me that refusal to drink under these circumstances was not an option. As Hibbert poured, Mills growled quietly in my ear, 'You have to knock it back in one swallow. Anything less is an insult. Understand, boy?'

I raised my glass to the captain's and gulped down the nastiness as instructed. My insides burned, my eyes watered. I fought a violent urge to vomit.

'You may leave us, sergeant.'

'But, cap'n!' Mills gestured at me. 'The black lad.'

'Yes, Mills?'

'I'm to leave you alone? With *him*?'

'Why, yes, man. To your duties now.'

'But Cap'n Hibbert, sir. He . . . he . . . he's *black*!'

'Evidently. Now go.'

Captain Hibbert slumped in his chair and stared at me for a very long time with an air of suppressed madness.

'Did he die well?'

'Who, sir?'

'The lad, Mr Hines.'

I declared that he had passed away nobly, in a

manner befitting a young gentleman.

'Did he cry out at all, or make any last requests?'

'He died like a young gentleman, captain. He had no last requests,' I lied, recalling the boys last distressed moments in this realm. By way of drawing attention away from any possible part I might have played in Hines's death I asked, 'Should we, the crew, I mean, the men – would you permit us to carry our commiserations to his family?'

'No young man. That would not be possible. You see his mother's life was taken in the most tragic and brutal circumstances, and his father is no longer the man he used to be.' He tapped his skull. 'Such news would serve no purpose for a man in his condition.'

To my horror he charged our glasses a second time with measures greater than the first.

'You've made quite a name for yourself since joining our crew, Black Prince. Your peculiar traits of strength, steadiness, ingenuity and obedience saved a great many lives yesterday. Clearly you are a boy of some education.'

I nodded gravely as if to confirm the truth of what he said.

'Take off your shirt and turn around!' he commanded.

I obeyed.

'Well, you're no slave as far as I can see.' He raised his voice above the racket of the carpenters bashing the ship back into shape. 'You have the makings of a good seaman, and more. I'm sure of it. We've many stalwart black fellows manning His Majesty's vessels. Damn fine sailors, the black tars.' He poured a third measure of rum for himself and one for me. He brandished the bottle. 'Jamaica rum. Good Jamaica rum, yes-o. I am from the island of Jamaica, you know. A Jamaican, that's what I am.'

Why he should wish to share this information with me was a mystery. Apart from a desire to see my fellow black people released from bondage, I had no interest at all in the Caribbean. I'd met a few people from Jamaica, mostly black, but some white, and they were pleasant enough fellows, if somewhat loud.

'I've always felt more at home with blacks around me. My wet nurse was a black woman.'

The image conjured by that detail so filled me with revulsion that I found myself unable to respond coherently to his next statement.

'Jupiter, I want you to agree to undertake a mission of the greatest urgency!'

He was starting to slur his words and had placed his hand on my shoulder, so by way of shortening my time in his company, I said, 'I will, sir!' giving no further consideration to his previous utterances.

'Excellent, excellent! It is of national, nay global, importance. Do you understand? I knew you wouldn't let me down.'

By now my shoulder was almost supporting his full weight and his red blowsy face was level with mine.

'I had wanted this mission to be the sole charge of my . . . my midshipman, Mr Hines, and one other, but with him gone I could think of nobody else aboard the *Boneta*, no one,' he swept an arm about him to encompass the ship, the ocean, the world, 'no one, no officer or deckhand better suited to the task I have in mind than yourself, Jupiter.'

'What task would that be, captain?' I looked at him pitifully, convinced he would ask me to act as a lookout in the topmast or something equally tedious.

'Have you ever heard of the Turtle, young man?'

I stated that I had. Once, a very long time ago, Patrick and I chanced upon a turtle when we were playing on a beach in Sierra Leone. It was heading inland for some reason and looked like it was a very long way away from home, so we turned it on its back and pulled it back to the sea to keep it from being killed and eaten.

'Erm, no. Not that sort of turtle, boy. I am referring to a submersible ship.'

'Begging your pardon, Captain Hibbert, but do you mean a ship that can travel below the surface of the ocean?' I looked from him to the bottle in his fist and back again.

'Yes, exactly!'

His face was mad and beaky like Mr Punch. He looked at me as if I held the secret to the universe. The way the truly insane sometimes do.

'If I understand you correctly, Captain Hibbert, is the crew of the *Boneta* about to embark on an adventure beneath the sea?' Recalling my topmast visions of mermaids and monsters, I struggled not to laugh.

'Not the crew exactly, Jupiter. *You* are. You and a second seaman.'

'Is that what you've been carrying in the hold? A submersible sea vessel?' He nodded excitedly. 'Dr Belloni will acquaint you with the principles behind its construction. He, together with Midshipman Hines, has expanded the original model to accommodate two sailors.'

'You say two it carries two sailors, captain . . .' I said, humouring him.

'Two, yes. The other would have been Mr Collett.

The lad, Mr Hines, wanted him to accompany him as he was his best friend. They were very close, you know. He would have found out about the honour of being chosen today, but as you know he is in no condition to carry out work of this kind now, is he?'

'Indeed not, sir.' I said, recalling the bandages I'd fixed to what remained of Collett's left hand.

'If I may be permitted to ask, captain, who shall be the second seaman?'

'Given the close quarters and degree of intimacy this mission will demand, I suggest it should be your own brother, Able Seaman Patrick Williams. He is said to be a good sailor and has some knowledge of navigation – which you do not.'

I felt compelled to voice my thanks, but before I could utter a word, Captain Hibbert added, 'In fact, I've already requested that he join us this evening.'

He poured two fresh measures.

'Thank you, sir.' I believe he was too drunk to notice that I had been tipping my rum into his chamber pot for the last two rounds.

I cleared my throat. 'Captain, sir, in the light of your requests may I venture to ask that, as a condition of my acceptance, my brother be spared the lashes he was awarded prior to our clash with the French frigate?'

He flicked his fingers at me like an elf-king sprinkling magic dust.

'Consider it done. Are you not daunted by the volume of knowledge the next two weeks will require you to take in?'

It had not occurred to me to that a body of mere facts, no matter how large, would prove difficult to absorb. But I sensed this was not the place for my immodesty. 'I dare say I will struggle through somehow, sir.'

He clutched the bottle as a child embraces a soft toy. 'I trust His Majesty's navy can count on you at this time, young man? Why, the Yankees gave one of their land soldiers only twenty days to familiarize himself with the machine, and he damn near sunk one of our flagships too. It goes without saying that one of Britannia's black tars can do better than a damn'd Yankee, eh?!'

Being lost for words and feeling only the need to exit the madman's cabin as quickly as possible, I shouted 'Aye, aye, sir!'

The main deck of the *Boneta* looked like a building site. The carpenter and his mates were busy all over the decks, masts and sides repairing broken yards and bunging holes. Their activity was compounded by a team of resourceful and nimble seamen who were repairing the huge wooden crane directly over the hold.

Rather than remaining below decks with my watch, I took a seat in one of the small launches and watched as the Turtle was brought up section by section from the hold and assembled on the deck below the crane. Soon the main deck was filled with gawpers of all ranks who had gathered to see this wonder. It took almost the entire afternoon before the completed vessel stood before us.

'Oh great God in Heaven!' It was Patrick. He had materialized beside me in the launch.

'I thought you didn't believe in him.'

'There's a time and place for everything, Jupiter. Now is a time for divine intervention, wouldn't you say?'

I nodded and looked at the Turtle. 'Is that it?' It looked like a giant hazelnut.

It was a seven-foot-high wooden oval reinforced with iron bands and wooden braces. I could make out the shape of what must have been a rudder and tiller at the back of the craft. There was a windowed hatch at the top, which I imagine allowed the pilot to peer into the world beneath the waters.

We both gulped audibly several times.

'Small, isn't it, Patrick?'

'Very. That looks like a very, very bad place to die.'

'Do you think that contraption is waterproof?'

'No.'

'This isn't a very good idea, is it? How do we get out of this one?'

'I have no idea. Perhaps we can feign illness.'

'Both of us? At the same time?'

'Well, one of us. You, for example.'

'Why, Patrick, you know I would never let you go off alone in that . . . thing! If you go, then so do I.'

'We have to go, Jupiter. Look at them.' Glancing up I realized we had become the centre of attention. All around us, along the masts, decks and rigging sailors were pointing at us, raising their caps, saluting and hallooing. 'The news must have spread throughout the ship. There's no turning back now.'

A voice from the mainmast bawled out: 'Three cheers for the Black Prince and Ol' Granny Williams! Hip-hip!'

Reluctantly we stood to accept their praise. They would have us as their heroes, whether we wanted it or not.

* * *

At four bells we gathered on deck to witness the burial at sea of our shipmates. The ship had stopped and the colours were displayed at half mast. I noted that all stations had been made ready; the firing squad, the casket bearers and the bugler. The bodies lay wrapped in canvas on planks positioned on the main deck. Lieutenant Glasgow passed the word aloud: 'All hands bury the dead!' and we came to parade rest. We stood bare-headed in the rain. The decks were soon wet and sloppy with the driving water and we stood there throughout an interminable burial service; the scripture, the prayers, the committal and the benediction. The firing squad raised their pieces and fired three times as each body was loosened to splash into the sea. I exchanged a look with Patrick as we watched the body of Midshipman Edward Hines go over the side. We knew that in two days' time we would be following his journey down into those same briny depths.

Whether we would ultimately rise or sink we knew not.

[10]

'Have you made up your reckoning, Mr Harding?' Captain Hibbert pushed the ship's master into his cabin and ushered us in behind him.

'I have, sir,' answered the master. 'If you will allow me.' He made an effort to spread out the chart on the captain's tiny writing table, but the paper was stiff from being almost continually rolled up. I stepped forward to grip two corners of the unruly sheet. The master sniffed at me. Patrick held the fourth corner.

'I want you to inform these two hands of your reckonings for the mission.'

Mr Harding looked at me and Patrick in turn. He sniffed twice and addressed Captain Hibbert.

'Well, sir, I've calculated our position for a launch here.' He pointed with his pencil to a dot surrounded by a tiny circle on the map. The circle was hard by the Moroccan coast. There was a date written alongside it: 14 April 1803. Ten days away. The two officers went on to discuss in exhaustive detail matters of 'allowance for leeway and drift while hove-to' and suchlike. I stared at that pencil mark. It represented us in seven days' time in a submarine, being set adrift on the open seas.

'The rules for this engagement are straightforward enough. We are to sink the flagship of the Sultan of Morocco. I don't suppose either of you have ever seen one of those grand old beauties, have you?'

'I have, sir,' Patrick ventured. 'They are something between Noah's Ark and the Lord Mayor's barge in size and taste, I would say.'

The captain looked at him as if for the first time.

'Are there any observations you would like to make, Able Seaman Williams?'

'Indeed, sir, begging your pardon. If we assume there'll be virtually no wind on the night, and clear but dark weather, and that the current is suitable, am I correct in thinking that we will approach the enemy ship with the windows of the Turtle just slightly above the level of the water and upon sighting her we descend, plunging into almost absolute darkness for nigh on twenty minutes, screw a weight of explosives into the hull and make good our return to a pre-arranged point.'

'You are indeed correct.'

'Permission to pose a question, sir?'

'Granted.'

'Correct me if I am wrong, sir, but to the best of my knowledge, we are not at war with the state of Morocco, are we?'

'Indeed, we are not. Apart from minor piracy, there is currently no quarrel between our two nations. But the United States of America is. We shall go about our business under the flag of Great Britain and we will attract little attention unless we open up with our big guns.'

'But we are at war with the French. Why do we not attack their fleets?'

'We will, we will soon enough. But first we need to make sure this turtle-machine actually works. We must determine where it fails and where it performs well.'

'You mean like an *experiment*,' I said, using a word I had learned from Robert, our younger brother.

'Exactly! If the machine works on the Moroccans, we will use it against the French. Imagine, an entire fleet of the things, roaming the globe unseen and striking terror into our enemies' hearts!'

He had that mad look in his eyes again and I gazed at my feet to avoid it.

Patrick proceeded to ask about speed, directions, rules of engagement, rate of knots and other things of which I was perfectly ignorant. I pretended to know what he was talking about and sent my scowl of informed concern along with his towards the captain.

'And now,' declared Captain Hibbert, 'let us cast rank aside and drink on this.'

I sighed heavily as he passed us drinks of yet more wretched rum. He held them with his fingers *inside* the three glasses in the English manner.

'God save the King!'

We repeated the toast, saluted and filed back to our quarters.

Dr Belloni was a filthy little man who could accurately be described as more blue-skinned than white.

'I take it, sir, that you are a native of Italy,' I said.

He raised himself to his full height of five feet and three inches. 'I am a native man of Sardinia.'

Belloni cared for neither freedom nor tyranny; Christian nor heathen, not for black men or white. He lived for knowledge alone. And money.

His personal habits were too foul to mention and they were made worse by his diet of dried sausage, milk and some awful devil-fart cheese called *cazu marzu*. The cheese (if such it can be called) was perfected by introducing flies' eggs into the mixture as it aged. It was deemed to be fit for human consumption when its consistency had been made mushy by colonies of maggots. Apparently the maggots were the best part, and knowing well our disgust, Belloni would wave scoops of the muck under our noses before slurping it up with theatrical relish.

'You come with me now!' he commanded. 'The Turtle pilot must be very strong and clever with good eyes. Which of you shall be him?'

'I shall,' said Patrick, stepping between me and Belloni. He shrugged my hand off his shoulder.

'Behold! The Turtle!' The Sardinian tapped the craft with a metal rod.

Close up, it looked so much smaller than I remembered. It seemed impossible that two large men could fit inside. We followed Belloni on to a small platform that had been built around the vehicle.

'You!' He pointed to me.

'My name is Jupiter, Dr Belloni!'

'Jupiter? A-ha, *Giove*!' He laughed, and as usual, I laughed along with the joke I'd heard a thousand times before in English.

'Jupiter, you enter first. Sit on the low seat under the high seat above it.' There were two tiny seats in the Turtle, one below the other. The upper seat was for the

110

pilot, who also worked a handle connected to a protruding screwlike bladed metal rod. Another screwlike blade was at the front. It would be my job to operate this.

Patrick climbed in after me and settled into position. It was very cramped indeed. I had to bend almost double to keep my head away from his backside.

'Am I expected to remain like this throughout the undersea journey?'

'*Si, si*. Yes, you make small yourself and work hard.'

I would have to maintain this posture while using the equipment. Thinking about such matters would drive me mad, so I asked the doctor to explain the principles behind the Turtle's operation.

'Is simple. I show you,' declared Belloni. 'You live, maybe. You die, maybe. Is war, yes?'

We could only agree.

'Is simple.' He tapped the rod on the handle built into the roof. 'Here, turn round the clock you go up. Against the clock you turn you go down.' He relit his cigar and pointed to the lower handle, the one that I would be working. 'To the clock you go forward, against the clock you go back. Is simple, no?'

It was simple. It would also be phenomenally hard work.

'It's very dark in here. How are we supposed to see what we are doing?'

'Have no fear. God has provided. Wait there.' He shouted for a marine to fetch him something. Presently he lowered a large glass jar to us. 'Let there be light! *Eco!*' The jar was full of floating, glowing lights: fireflies.

We were shown a foot-operated valve and a water pump to admit and discharge water from inside the vehicle (though why we would want to let water into the Turtle was beyond me). The Sardinian instructed us in the use of the water gauges, the barometer, the compass and the ventilator, in case we needed to snorkel.

'Now for this, you must listen. Is very important. If the ship she sink. You pull the chain in the floor.'

We stared at him.

'Lead,' he said.

We blinked at him.

'Lead, the metal. Nine hundred pounds of the metal, lead. They come out the bottom and to the top of the sea you rise like balloon. You live.' Using the stub of his cigar he demonstrated our ascent. We blinked at him some more. 'Is ballast, you see. For if you have emergency. If the Turtle she go down with violence you may levitate to the level of the sea and survive.'

* * *

At first it felt wonderful to be relieved of our old duties. There would be no more sore knees from scrubbing the decks. There would be no more sore and grubby fingers from endlessly polishing brass fittings till they gleamed or blackening the ship's guns. Our whole existence was much more agreeable. We were eating better food. No more dolphin and dumpling, but we ate from the officers' menu as much salt beef, plum duff and lime juice as we could devour, and more. Our sleeping arrangements changed and we left our old messes to be quartered together in the hold, which, despite the noxious presence of Dr Belloni, afforded us much greater space and almost eight hours of sleep every night.

On the second day of this routine Francis came to visit us.

'So, you're really going, then?'

'It would seem so,' I said.

'I know it's bad luck to wish good luck, but . . . but . . .'

The young man burst into tears and rushed forward to embrace us. Patrick despised these displays of affection and held him at bay. I flung a comforting arm over his shoulder.

'I'm going to miss you, Jupiter!' he snivelled. 'I wish I could come with you.'

'No you don't. This is a journey from which we may never return,' barked Patrick. 'I wouldn't wish that on my worst enemy.'

'But you will return though. I know you will. Nothing can defeat the Williams family, can it?'

Patrick and I looked at one another and only just failed to temper our swelling pride. *Nothing could defeat us!*

'I owe you so much, Jupiter,' Francis continued. 'If it hadn't been for you, I might still be a sad little houseboy living by Clapham Common and never seeing a soul, let alone another black face. But I have a life now, don't I?'

Patrick nodded. 'A seaman's life can be yours, if that's what you want. You make friends easily and are prepared to apply yourself. I have no doubt you may even rise to petty officer rank, in due time. The world is yours, or at least its oceans are.'

'But what I want most of all is to go to Africa, to Sierra Leone, after everything you've told me about it.'

'Well, young Francis,' I said as I extended my hand to shake his, 'maybe we will meet you there one of these days. Stranger things have happened.'

'God go with you, Jupiter! God go with you too, Patrick!'

We started to enjoy our new regime under Dr Belloni. We warmed to him and gradually came to comprehend his bizarre ways with the English language. We liked it that he seemed to treat us as if we were normal people and worked us accordingly. His behaviour was devoid of that atrocious beaming many educated English folk display when they discover black people can count beyond three. Or maybe he just hadn't learned to say 'black bastard' in English yet. Either way, our time with him was a delight. We learned quickly and thoroughly.

It was brutally hard training nonetheless. I hadn't realized there would be a physical side to our instruction. At least three hours of every day were spent raising and lowering cannon balls of various weights and running on the spot at great speed or performing countless press-ups. But I was comfortable with all that. What I dreaded were the lessons in navigation and steering. The Sardinian could not have had a worse pupil. I am by no means slow-witted, and I believe I can master most subjects, but plotting a course through water, making use of changing currents, land masses, using the positions of stars and so on, was something I found supernaturally boring. The simplest ideas were made obscure beneath layer after layer of seafaring jargon. Patrick, of course, loved all of that nautical nonsense, and as he had elected himself as pilot discussed these matters at considerable length with Belloni. Indeed, Patrick seemed to be the only one discussing things with Belloni. Captain Hibbert had gifted this mission to me in regard for my talents, but here was my big brother elbowing me aside and leaving me to work my propellers round-and-around-and-round-and-around-and-round like a dumb ox grinding corn.

As the principal pilot Patrick was also given the task of fixing the explosive charge to the sultan's flagship. If the mission was a success, he would claim all the glory. But as the time of our departure drew near, I was less and less concerned with 'glory'. It was all I could do to concentrate on the simple tasks I was set, for fear of my own death had beset me.

In my brief time on this earth, I have come close to losing my life on a few occasions. Whether falling from a height, drowning or being shot, my days might have ended suddenly. Now, on a ship full of clocks, bells and timepieces I was horribly aware of my doom's steady, ticking arrival. And so it was that I found myself, on our last night on board the *Boneta* on my knees, deeply in prayer. Naturally, I prayed that if our lives were lost on this mission, we would spend eternity with our heavenly father. The prospect of meeting our earthly father there as well gave me added comfort. I prayed for our younger brother Robert, that he would continue to prosper and to cultivate his gift of great intelligence. I prayed that he would soon make his way from London back to Sierra Leone and continue our family's work there. I prayed especially for Patrick, my brother the unbeliever. Patrick, who had renounced all religion, would need all the prayer-power I could muster to save his soul from eternal damnation. Mid-prayer I raised my head and looked over to where he was sitting cross-legged on the floor ticking and ruling his way through a sheaf of maps. His faith was in the wisdom of men. Mine was in a higher power.

We were honoured to dine as the guests of Captain Hibbert on our last evening. 'Eat heartily now, boys. You may take this meal as a reminder of how close we are to land,' he joked.

We were eating roast seagulls. Francis, in his role as cabin boy, carved and served the birds for us. It felt very odd to have Francis standing in silence behind us as we ate what could possibly be our last meal alive. As I feared, Patrick and the captain drank somewhat heavily and quickly before falling into old sea-dog stories and rank was temporarily ignored. I shared an occasional look of consolation with Francis while chewing mouthfuls of seagull. I listened to the bell clanging a change of watch on deck, the comforting rumble of fifty pairs of feet rushing to their duties, all the jests and bad language, the sound of harmonicas played terribly, and from every part of the ship, the creaking strain of ropes and timbers. I was going to miss it all very much.

'Young man.' The captain cleared his throat. 'Our talk of the high seas and gruff men seems to bore you. I would have thought you would be most keen to advance your knowledge of naval matters.'

'Indeed I am, Captain Hibbert. I was merely reflecting on how much I will miss the *Boneta* and her crew.'

'Miss? Miss us? Why, man, you will not miss us, for you shall return victorious. I swear that by three bells in the seven dog watch at the very latest you will be back on board.'

'Would you be meaning half past seven, captain?' I asked.

'Half past seven it is.'

Why didn't you say that then? I thought. Why does everything in the navy have to be so roundabout? *Why*?

Captain Hibbert stood. We rose immediately to join him.

'In rendering this sterling service to the nation, you are putting yourself in a most favourable light. Upon my honour, Jupiter.' I was startled. He had addressed me by my first name. 'I am not without influence in either the Admiralty or the Jamaica station. Within the year I expect to be wearing the braid of an admiral.' He stood up and offered me his hand. 'And you, Mr Williams, will be sponsored as a midshipman under my command. That I promise you.'

I was so taken aback by this pronouncement that I took an overly large swig of wine. 'Thank you, sir. From the bottom of my heart, I thank you most sincerely,' I slurred.

The words 'Midshipman Jupiter Williams' repeated over and over in my ears until it was as if a choir of angels was singing to my success. I imagined myself cutting a dashing figure in my middy's uniform with its stiff collar, all black and gold braid as I yelled orders through my speaking-trumpet.

Midshipman Jupiter Williams.

'Regrettably,' Captain Hines turned to Patrick, 'your age is against you and I could not offer you a similar position, but every ship needs a good bosun's mate, and you, Patrick Williams, would be one of the very best. Of that I am sure.'

Patrick grunted and half-saluted. 'Aye, sir!'

'Gentlemen!' said the captain, snapping to attention. 'Go now to your duties!'

'Aye, aye, sir!' we chorused.

Francis accompanied us out, past the marine sentry and into the corridor. He was more excited than I was. He hopped up and down and patted me on the back whooping all the while. 'Midshipman, eh? Wow. A midshipman. Whoo!' And so he continued as we made our way through the ship saying our last farewells.

'Captain seems to have taken quite a shine to you, doesn't he?' grumbled Patrick.

'It would seem so. It must be on account of that rotten tooth I drew from his mouth. It must have caused him great pain.'

'A tooth, you say? Do you really think you are in his favour because of his bad teeth? Think, Jupiter! Just open your eyes and think hard for once in your life. There's a big clue right there.'

'Where?'

'Bad teeth!' He stormed away, shaking his head.

I was confused. It is true that in rejoicing at my own good fortune, I had not spared a thought for my brother, the future bosun's mate. He was, by any standard, the better sailor and my indifference to navigation was a source of embarrassment to him. Could jealousy have driven him to make such irrational remarks about *bad teeth*?

I shook off these considerations and made my way to see Dr Druce. The surgeon was standing alone holding on to the rail on the poopdeck. His eyes were bound with a fresh cloth I had applied two days ago.

'Ah, Jupiter!'

'How did you know it was me, Dr Druce?'

'By your footstep. So determined and yet so uncertain. It really is quite singular.'

'I have great news, doctor.'

'So the time has come for you to embark on your undersea adventure?'

'Yes, sir. And there's more. Upon my return, Captain Hibbert has sworn to sponsor me as a midshipman!'

'Has he now?' Dr Druce stroked his chin. 'And you have accepted the proposition, I take it?'

'Aye, gladly.'

'Oh.'

'Are you not pleased for me, sir?'

'I am, of course. But have you not considered any other future for yourself, apart from the navy?'

'I love the sea, Dr Druce. I love all of this,' I said, gesturing at the ship he could no longer see. 'Also there are many of my people serving on His Majesty's ships. It would do them a world of good to see one of their own wearing some gold braid.'

'Hmm. Your people may well need naval officers, Jupiter. But they need other kinds of leaders as well.'

'You mean men of politics, business and the Church. No, sir, I am not one of those sort—'

'No, Jupiter. I mean men of medicine. They need doctors.' He held out his hand. 'Think on this, promise me.'

'I shall think on it, doctor, I promise you.' But as I shook his hand and bade him farewell it was images of flashing gold braid, a black uniform and new, polished shoes that filled my mind.

When I arrived on the main deck I found the crew standing at ease under the crane around the Turtle. Dr Belloni was among them. It was one of the few times I'd seen the Sardinian in fresh air. Patrick was already there, by the side of the submarine. A tiny bag of personal items lay at his feet. He had an impatient look on his face. Sentimental goodbyes amongst fully-grown men were not at all to his taste.

'Jupiter!' he commanded. 'Let's be away!' Patrick nodded up at Lieutenant Glasgow and the captain on the poopdeck. We touched where our forelocks would have been had we been white men and prepared to enter the craft. I went first, lowering myself into the bottom half of the submarine. It was unbelievably dark and only my familiarity with the parts of the vessel gave me some idea of where I was and what I was supposed to be doing. I could hear Mr Harding addressing Dr Belloni in what I understood to be a mishmash of bad French and worse Spanish. In anticipation of my brother clambering into position I pressed myself into the side of the Turtle as much as possible. Patrick seemed to take up an excessive amount of room. He was practically standing on my shoulders for a while. Eventually he sat down and my discomfort changed from atrocious to merely harsh.

'Don't forget these now!' The voice belonged to Sergeant Mills. The jar of fireflies was passed down to us to turn our darkness to twilight. 'Nor these.' Sergeant Mills handed over a brace of service pistols.

'They're loaded. In case you get captured alive by the enemy. Not that you will, of course.'

'Not that they'll do us much good either!' I snapped back. 'They're useless. Just like you! Only one ball in—'

Whether the sergeant was nodding or shaking his head as he slammed the roof shut I didn't really know or care.

We heard Belloni outside, huffing and puffing as he checked all the seals. There was a rough shudder and almost a fall as we felt the clamps being attached. After a while, the Turtle lurched briefly before being winched from the deck, swung overboard and lowered into the water. The temperature inside the Turtle dropped the moment we entered the water. We did not just enter it, we fell, and kept on falling. It could only have been for a matter of seconds, but it felt like an eternity. We were supposed to float, and float we did. The Turtle bobbed back to the surface with surprising grace.

A pair of lowered barges were waiting to row us out into position. The clamps were released and new lines were attached to the barges. Craning my neck upwards, I could see my brother working the controls with maniacal focus. His face was lit up by torches from the barges shining through the pilot's window.

As the oarsmen stroked us away from the *Boneta* they sang:

'I thought I heard the old man say
Goodbye, fare ye well,
Goodbye, fare ye well.
I thought I heard the old man say,
Hooray, my boys, we're homeward bound.

We're homeward bound, I hear the sound.
Goodbye, fare ye well,
Goodbye, fare ye well.
We're homeward bound, I hear the sound.
Hooray, my boys, we're homeward bound.

And soon we'll be ashore again.
Goodbye, fare ye well,
Goodbye, fare ye well
And soon we'll be ashore again.
Hooray, my boys, we're homeward bound.'

[*12*]

Patrick, the gallant self-appointed pilot-commander-supreme, had the easier part of the work. I had to work the horizontal propeller with my left hand and steer the submarine with my right hand, all the while keeping an eye on the compass to guide us to the hull of the enemy ship. Patrick, in the meantime, was just sitting pretty staring out of the window.

'I estimate we've travelled one and a half miles to target. What say you, landman?'

I didn't like the change of tone in Patrick's voice. I thought I was his brother. When did I become just a landman to him? 'Well, you are the great navigator. I suppose you must be correct.'

The effort of keeping the machine going was extremely fatiguing. I must have turned the propeller through several thousand rotations. There was absolutely no appreciable sense of forward motion whatsoever. I breathed shallowly, little and often, as Dr Belloni had taught us and focused on the task at hand. Anything rather than considering the fact that we were underwater on the edge of the Mediterranean heading towards Morocco with a charge of explosives in a craft that had not yet been proved to work.

'I shall soon commence the pumping out of ballast water,' Patrick continued, 'and we shall presently descend to a depth of five feet where we will stabilize the vessel and continue on course.'

'Aye. Sir!' I snapped mockingly.

Patrick worked his handle with surprising vigour and in moments the water closed over our heads and our view was pitch-black save for the feeble lights emitted by our insects. The temperature dropped more shockingly still. I worked on to keep warm.

'Jupiter, pass me that map!' Patrick gestured with his foot.

'Patrick, I beg you not to address me in that way. I am not your servant.'

'True, you are not my servant, but you are only a landman. I am an able seaman and I outrank you here.'

'But the captain chose *me* for this mission. And I accepted you. Therefore I have seniority!' I protested.

'Seniority! He only picked you because you remind him of that Hines boy. The boy you *allowed to die*, remember?'

I could not believe Patrick said such a thing. During

our time at sea my muscles had grown as rapidly as my patience had shrunk. I could have bested him in a struggle, to be sure, but this was not the place for it, instead I used my anger to power the Turtle forward with greater speed.

'We will maintain this speed for the next twenty minutes,' he commanded.

I worked silently and steadily. After a while, Patrick leaned down from his seat and gave me a hand. As he helped turn the screw he sang one of those old Jamaican tunes we used to love so much.

> *Wherever de army go, Satan follow*
> *Satan follow, wherever de army go*

We were making good speed and were now quite warm in our little cabin. Without external light or points of reference it was hard to measure the passage of time. Every time Patrick checked his fob-watch barely one minute had passed. We needed more songs.

We tried traditional Sierra Leonean songs we had picked up during our trading missions with Father upriver, but they failed to raise our spirits. Inevitably we found refuge in the tunes the Jamaicans had brought to the country: the music our father detested. We sang 'Devil mek you must behave so bad!', a song

Father once beat us for singing. He beat us loudly enough for our wails to be heard all over Freetown and the following Sunday he gave a sermon on the matter to a packed church.

'Hey, Jupiter! Remember that other song we used to sing all the time, "Long Time"? How did it go again?'

> *Long time now me would a chop off him hand*
> *Run, Mabel, bring the good machete come*
> *Long time now me would a tief de bwoy land*
> *Run, Mabel, bring the good machete come*

Our work at the propeller soon failed in a flurry of laughter. Patrick was half out of his seat, and I was leaning over my controls trying to hold myself together.

'Enough laughter, my brother.' Patrick straightened himself in the pilot's seat. 'We must get back to work. We will fall behind.'

But I couldn't stop laughing. Our situation was crazy.

'Jupiter, I beg you. We need to conserve our supply of air. Remember what Dr Belloni said. Stop laughing now. And you can stop tickling me as well.' I suppressed my mirth but I could not stop tickling Patrick because both my hands were busy. I had one hand on the rudder and the other on the horizontal screw.

'Stop that at once, Jupiter! Jupi— *Awwuuuurghhh eeleiwrah!*' screamed Patrick.

A rat the size of a bad wig scuttled up the wall and hung shivering on the ceiling inches above Patrick's head.

My brother exploded instantly in every imaginable direction.

Imagine a fight in a cupboard. No, imagine a fight in a coffin. Underwater. Patrick was making so much noise, I feared he might be heard in Tangiers harbour.

I wrapped my arms and legs about him, and using all my strength, I tried to keep him from destroying the submarine, striking me or breaking the firefly jar which had been knocked to the floor.

My brother had broken out in terribly profuse sweating, like a fever victim. He was fighting for breath and his eyeballs were bulging and flicking all about in a most disturbing manner. I could sense the elemental power of his fear, but I could not let his fear infect me. It was only a rat, after all. Less than one-sixteenth of his size, and yet it could reduce him to a quivering wreck and endanger a mission of national importance.

I was about to start giggling at the ludicrousness of the situation when Patrick's eyes rolled back into his skull and he stopped breathing. It was now my turn to panic. I let Patrick drop to the floor and pressed back his eyelids, as if the sight of his eyeballs would somehow restore his health. I began to pray aloud. I invoked the help of the Almighty in this our hour of direst need. In no time at all I was babbling deliriously and beside myself. This couldn't be the time and place of our death. Not here, like this. No, we were the Williams family. Suddenly before my eyes swam the faces of our mother and father. They were looking at us with patience, great strength and kindness. This was no ordinary prayer. It had the substance of fact. It was as if our tiny nutshell of a boat had expanded and about us swam faces. Faces like ours, the faces of our ancestors, those who had given birth in time of war, in time of famine, on board a slave ship. Those who didn't die. They were all with us as we struggled to breathe and work another turn of the handle and fight another day. Wordlessly, they spoke to me and through me they spoke to Patrick.

We are Williams
We were Africans
We could not be defeated
We were taken from Africa and enslaved
We survived the journey

In the hold of a slave ship
Across the Atlantic
There were rats on the slave ship too. And more
We could not be defeated
We survived slavery in America
We fought slavery in America
We fled America to Canada
We survived Canadian winters and prospered
We could not be defeated
We returned to Africa
We prospered
We are still here
And through us, our ancestors are still here.
We are all here.
We will not die here.

As I finished this strangest of incantations, my brother shook his head once, blinked himself to consciousness and took a very deep breath as if he had endured nothing more than a short nap. He sat up sharply through ninety degrees like a man possessed and calmly climbed back into his seat. I was speechless.

'We will continue our mission. Jupiter, check the compass,' he said in a flat voice. Miraculously, the reading was but a few degrees off our true course. 'Two degrees tacking north, north-east, Patrick. Rudder adjusted accordingly. We'll be back on course before you know it.'

We continued in absolute silence for several minutes. 'Where's the rat?' he asked in the same dead tones.

'It's right here beside me. I can see it. It's not moving, or anything.'

'That's fine. That's just fine.'

'Do you want me to kill it?'

Patrick shook his head. He was scaring me. I think I preferred him when he was old Granny Williams. At least he was recognizable.

'Leave the rat. Right now we have work to do.'

'Work to do? What do you mean?'

'Because we are here.'

'Indeed we are.' I spoke to him as I would to an idiot. 'We *are* both here. You and me. We are here.'

'I mean we are here. We have arrived. We are in the port.'

'How do you know this?'

'We must be. Listen.'

Sure enough, above the wash of the waters, we heard ship-noises; the clanking of chain, the creaking of old timbers. There was also the noise and motion of our little stowaway, of course, and it is to my brother's credit that he managed to hold his concentration and rise above his fears.

The increased rise and fall of our little craft informed us that we were under a very large ship.

'We are in the port and beneath a vessel of considerable size. But how do we know it is the right ship? The flagship?'

My brother wiped the sweat from his forehead and flicked his chin at the fireflies. 'Right ship, wrong ship? That is not our concern now, little brother. We have made it into the port, that's good enough for me and good enough for the Admiralty. Let's just drill this charge into whatever we may be under and get away before we suffocate.'

He began to furiously wind the vertical propeller clockwise to bring the submarine into contact with the hull. Once he felt certain that he was in place, he worked the drill into the bottom of the hull. It made a dreadful racket, like scratching fingernails down a blackboard. The Turtle rattled with each turn of the screw. The racket went on for ever.

'There!' he declared. 'It is done. I shall now detach the auger and release the magazine.'

'Aye, aye, captain,' I whispered with unfeigned reverence.

The release mechanism made a noise that could have woken the dead. Nothing in our training had prepared us for this.

'And what now?'

'We wait.'

'Wait here? For what? Can't we wait somewhere else?'

'The charge is timed. We must wait a full five minutes before we can depart.'

The rat was sitting upright on the floor by my feet and staring directly at me. At a loss for anything else to do I held the animal's gaze. I had been looking at it for a while before I realized that I was feeling quite drowsy. I was close to concluding that the creature had put me under some spell when I noticed the cabin was somewhat gloomier than before. Only a few fireflies were still alive in the jar. Our supply of air was running out.

'Patrick, forget about the full charge. We are losing air. We need to leave now!'

'No, Jupiter.' He was back to his normal pilot-supremo self. 'We will wait another three minutes.'

'Can't we use the snorkel?'

'It may have escaped your notice that we are directly beneath an object that would render the snorkel useless. Besides, we must dive sharply to distance ourselves from the explosion.'

I silently counted out one hundred and eighty seconds before giving a signal to disengage.

'I am commencing our descent now.' He started an anticlockwise winding motion. 'On the count of three, you will propel us away and steer us on a course of eight degrees south, south-east.'

We worked our propellers like madmen. This time our efforts were so concerted we actually felt the little submarine jerking downwards through the water.

We tired quickly and Patrick ordered me to rest. 'The bomb should have gone off by now,' he said.

'Did you hear an explosion?'

He shook his head. 'No. Did you?' He looked as if he too was fighting sleep. 'It must have gone off. That was a lot of gunpowder. We should have at least felt the waves from the shock. Remember what Belloni said.'

We didn't hear a *boom*. In fact we could barely hear anything. The air seemed thicker and heavier than usual inside the Turtle. Patrick's voice, and my own, sounded further away as if we were communicating through half a mile of pipe. My ears were ringing.

136

My head hurt. 'Patrick, the barometer! How far down are we?'

The barometer was not even bobbing at its lowest reading.

I tried to inhale, but found I could not. We had run out of air.

We were sinking. In our exhaustion we had left the Turtle to the mercies of the currents. The fireflies faded into a darkness so intense as to seem a weight.

'The water . . . the excess water . . . use the pump . . . must get to the surface . . . no . . . more air!'

We pumped until we lost all strength, and in my panicked state I imagined the rat pumping out water alongside us.

'The chain, Patrick. I must pull the chain and release the lead!'

The last thing I remembered was fixing my fingers slowly about those rusty metal links and pulling them with me as I collapsed into unconsciousness.

[*13*]

I saw clouds, lots of clouds in very bright sunlight when I came to. They appeared to be floating beneath me and I felt an urge to walk on them, but I could not move. I was at the threshold of Heaven, surely!

'Jupiter, Jupiter, can you hear me?'

It was my brother calling from somewhere out of view, perhaps calling me to Heaven's gate itself. 'Jupiter?'

It was only when his head appeared between my feet and the clouds that I understood that I had been asleep at the bottom of the Turtle. The hatch was thrown open and Patrick was sitting in it, dangling his feet over the side.

'Are you hungry?'

I was ravenous.

Patrick had a crust of bread and some hard blackened beef that tasted of gunpowder. We wolfed it down. Almost immediately we were attacked by the most pressing thirst. So I did that thing which even the greenest sailor knows not to do. I did the very thing most guaranteed to cause distress in that situation. I drank sea water. I drank long and deep of it. It did not taste all that bad, I must say. Admittedly, it was very salty (but then I have always been most partial to salty foods) but it went down well enough and slaked my thirst to such an apparent degree that I eventually managed to persuade my brother, the old sea-dog, to follow my example.

Within the hour we were vomiting like plague victims. At first we expelled solids, next came fluids (and I had no idea my body contained so much liquid stuff. It was never-ending). At last, out came the air, in long, bellowing burps, until all that remained within us was the animating spark of the Holy Spirit, and even that we now desired to extinguish, so that we could be free from the torments of this world.

The day was hot. When I say it was hot, I mean it was hot in the extreme. So hot, in fact, that pitch boiled out from the seams of the Turtle and all its iron fittings and stanchions were too hot to hold or rest against for longer than two seconds at a time. It was so hot that we had to fold fabric of all kinds about the vessel simply so we could lean against it in the strong sunlight. Patrick perched on the lip of the Turtle, the better to increase the space between himself and the rat that lurked below. The sun beat down on my unprotected head so relentlessly that I was quite delirious with a headache. My saliva was now thick and foul-tasting. My tongue had become as dry as old leather. It was swollen and stuck to my teeth and the roof of my mouth like that of an imbecile. I felt my senses departing one by one. My strength was sinking fast, until all I knew of this mortal realm was the sound of my own shallow breathing.

Suddenly, bubbling around the edges of the Turtle, came flurries of slim, silver flying fish. They leaped from the water and arced through the air. They sparkled high and made beautiful patterns. My dulled mind was so enraptured by these visions that it was some minutes before it dawned upon me that I was looking at food and, what was more, *drink*. I removed my shirt and fashioned it into a crude net. The sea was so alive with the creatures that it took only three simple trawls through the water to dredge six fish on board.

We fell upon the flapping, wriggling fish and greedily sucked out their blood and ate their raw flesh. And as we ate the poor fish alive, I recalled some words from the Bible, from the book of Leviticus: *These shall ye eat of all that are in the waters: whatsoever hath fins and scales in the waters, in the seas, and in the rivers, them shall ye eat.*

We ate like ogres and we looked like them too, gurgling greedily with a mess of blood and entrails dripping from our chins to our chests.

Later, gazing out across the vastness of the ocean, I experienced an awful sinking of the heart when it occurred to me that these could be our last moments upon the earth. No one would ever know anything about our fate. We could die unmourned. How great a number of the humankind die unmourned? How greater is the number that lie in the earth and under the sea unremembered. Suddenly I felt closer to my brother than I had ever felt to any human being.

'Patrick, I was reflecting on a set of possibilities that I trust you'll not think too far-fetched.'

'Far-fetched.' He looked about him. 'More far-fetched than *us here*?'

'Well, I have been drawing comparisons of some relative similarities of behaviour and physiognomy between the dead midshipman, Mr Hines, and Captain Hibbert. Could it conceivably be the case that they are related … that they are in fact father and son?'

My brother shook his head and looked at me as if wholly dazed. 'Why, Jupiter, it is more than a notion, it was common knowledge throughout the ship and the constant gossip of the crew. Why did you think his fellow midshipmen disliked him so? Because his skin was black? Because he had money? Everyone in Jamaica knows the story. When Sergeant Mills was stationed there he heard all about it, too.'

I ignored the feeling of stupidity that threatened to reduce me to tears and settled down to hear the tale.

'Mr Hines's mother was a black woman.'

'I can see *that*!'

'No, I mean she was a slave. She went by the name of Maria. She was one of a package of lives sold to one of the Hibbert plantations. The captain was a young man at the time, maybe sixteen or seventeen years old. He lost his heart to her and a child, a boy, was born of their union. Now, that sort of thing happens regularly on the plantations between master and slave, as I'm sure you can imagine. Most often, the fathers will sell their own children as if they were a chair or a wardrobe. Occasionally, the children are given their liberty. The young Maurice Hibbert doted on the boy and naturally set him and the mother free.

'Some six years later, Maria, the boy's mother was found dead. She had been murdered, found hanging from a tree. Burned her, they did. Cut her badly too.

Nasty. Problem was, the captain was a married man at the time. He'd been married two years before to the daughter of another of Jamaica's big trading families. He had no choice in the matter. His wife was a jealous one. Mad jealous. The whole island knew about Maurice and Maria and she didn't like it, being the laughing stock of Kingston high society. Her people and the Hibberts are the richest in the land, you see. Maria's child was sent away to England. Put in the care of a discreet family friend. A vicar in Shropshire, or somewhere. To this day, Captain Maurice Hibbert is still married in law to the same woman who murdered his mistress, and there are those that say that is why our esteemed first officer took to the sea in the first place. Would that we could all live so cursed, eh? Edward Hines, though motherless and without a father's instruction, grew up in a fashion to which only the most elevated of England's aristocrats have been accustomed. He was given the story that his parents had died in a terrible carriage accident in Jamaica, which resulted in him being sent to London as the sole heir of the estate. In terms of education, nothing was denied him. He was tutored privately by the finest minds trained in the most rigorous disciplines. He was escorted across Europe on the Grand Tour, in the style of England's favoured sons.'

'And Captain Hibbert,' I asked, 'did he not see his only son again until they served together on the *Boneta*?'

'Of course he did. The Hibberts are a family of enormous influence in London as well as Kingston. They straddle the Atlantic. Whenever our captain showed his face in Shropshire it was under the guise of a "family friend", some concerned soul bringing news and gifts from the island of the child's birth. How strange for him to have been reared in England. Always the only black face almost everywhere he went.'

'And of course,' I added, 'when Maurice Hibbert went to sea, it was natural that "as a friend of the family" he'd want to sponsor Edward Hines too.'

As we drifted along, I reflected on my own time in England and how, at times, even though I was schooled with others of my race in London, I had felt so incredibly alone. I could not imagine how it must have been for Edward Hines to grow up in the middle of the countryside surrounded entirely by white people.

We floated on from nowhere to nowhere.

'So, able seaman? Where are we then?'

'I shall tell you in a moment.'

Patrick unfolded the map, examined a section

of it and scribbled figures into a corner. He brought up the compass, refolded a section of the map and took a compass reading.

'Well?' I asked. 'I don't know, Jupiter. I need to do some more calculations.'

We bobbed along through a sleepless night, thankful only for the absence of the sun, but morning brought us round to face the full force of the great star again. This time, it was so hot we had to take shelter from the sun's rays within the Turtle and close the hatch after us, taking care to submerge the vessel from time to time.

When the air grew too foul we surfaced and broke the hatch on the submarine. It felt like stepping from a larder into an oven. Although I had been to sea before, it took a voyage in something the size of the Turtle to remind you of the ocean's vastness. We floated then submerged, floated then submerged. Occasionally Patrick took a look at the weather, the map or his watch, but it was clear that his readings were more of a ritual than an act of navigation. Whenever he studied, the rat would appear and sidle up to him as if to join him in scrutiny of the charts. Patrick was so absorbed or exhausted that he made no effort to bat it away.

'He likes you,' I teased. 'He needs a name, don't you think?'

After two days afloat, some kind of truce had been made between my brother and the rat. He started to feed him scraps of fish. By hand. 'I'll call him Rupert. Yes, Rupert.'

I think I preferred when my brother was an enemy to rodents to this unseemly closeness.

On our third morning of torment, just as I was about to close the hatch and send the submarine down into the cooling waters, Patrick stayed my hand.

'Look!' He indicated sea and then more sea. 'Look, can you see it?' I could see little clearly in such bright sunshine, but he insisted. 'Look, Jupiter, there, a-heading straight across our course astern! I swear it's a brig.'

His sailor-speak was gibberish to me, but I gazed into the distance where he pointed. I could distinguish nothing but sea and sky with patches of white cloud speckling the horizon. My heart sank from the belief that my brother had mistaken one of these for the sheen of a distant sail. We had to submerge before we were roasted alive. Then, as our vessel was suddenly flung higher on the crest of a great wave, my straining

146

eyes caught the unmistakable ripple of canvas.

'I see it! It's from America,' I said as its colours came into view. 'What is a Yankee brig doing so close to Africa?'

Patrick exchanged a despairing look with the rat.

A flash from the deck alerted us to a spyglass being trained in our direction.

'They're all up in the rigging, changing tack. They're coming to get us!'

I primed and cocked both pistols and passed one to Patrick.

Even a slave ship has water on board.

Patrick squinted at the letters painted in gold on the ship's side. 'The *Traveller*,' he read.

I shook my head in wonder. 'The *Traveller*? That *Traveller*? Here?'

Patrick knew this ship. All informed black people had heard of it. The *Traveller* was the vessel belonging to the richest black man in the Americas; the trader Captain Paul Cuffe. And there returning our wave as we bobbed into view were the black faces of its crew.

One face in particular drew our attention. It was beardless, unlike the others. It smirked.

'Oh, hello,' he said as hands reached over to haul us aboard.

We caught the bulwarks and rigging of the vessel, and in the next moment were rolled on to the deck and lay there panting.

Our little brother Robert stepped forward to greet us as if nothing very remarkable at all had just occurred.

With a hand on each of our shoulders he solemnly informed us: 'So we are going home, at last. My brothers, we are going home.'

[*14*]

For a moment I was sure I was looking at Father standing behind Robert. But it was not Father. Father was dead. The man who held my attention was none other than Paul Cuffe himself; Cuffe the trader, Cuffe the whaler, Cuffe the preacher and farmer. It seemed as if all successful black men carried themselves with the same gravity, were equally chubby and wore the same fixed frown.

'Ah, what sweet reunion. And you,' he said to Patrick, 'you must be . . . it can't be . . . why, yes, it's little Patrick. You were yay-high when last I saw you on your father's knee.' Although Patrick now stood considerably taller than him, he insisted on patting his head.

Patrick was incapable of returning the greeting. Like me, he was rendered speechless by the presence of our brother Robert. But it was impossible! I touched my little brother's face and hands, desperate to make the moment less unreal. Patrick did the same. It did not help matters.

'Robert, is that you?'

'Yes, Jupiter. It is me, Robert. Isn't this fantastic? Aren't you happy to see me?'

I was certain I would be overjoyed, once I was over the shock of seeing him in the flesh. 'What are you doing here? In the middle of the ocean? Why aren't you still in London? How on earth did you manage to find us?'

'Please, Jupiter, not now. First let us give thanks!'

'An excellent suggestion!' declared Captain Cuffe.

He grasped our hands and indicated that we should each link with another to close a circle of prayer. Patrick exhaled audibly and flicked his eyes skywards.

'Oh Lord,' called Captain Cuffe, 'as your servant Jonah was rescued from the belly of the whale so has Providence seen fit to deliver unto our safekeeping Patrick and . . . and . . . what's your name, young man?'

'Jupiter,' I croaked. I could have murdered for a sip of water.

'To deliver Patrick and Jupiter into our safekeeping. We pray that through the suffering which they have borne with fortitude they will submit to severer trials under the sanction of your higher teaching. We pray that the courage and steadfastness of our brave crew may receive an accession of energy from the example of hope that is set before them, and that your guiding hand may clear a way to return these wandering sons of Afric' to their—'

Patrick groaned.

'Speak, Patrick,' Captain Cuffe declaimed. 'Bear witness to—'

Patrick collapsed.

'Water, bring water instantly!'

We gulped all that was carried before us and asked for more.

'Your father was a very wonderful man. I never knew your mother, but from what I heard of her character, I am sure she is smiling down from Heaven upon you.'

We grunted and kept on slurping until our stomachs were at the point of bursting.

'You are making a most timely return to Sierra Leone. Indeed your presence there will greatly benefit the rise of—'

A huge burp tore its way out of my stomach before I could stop it.

Robert cleared his throat. 'Captain Cuffe, forgive my brothers. Their privations have reduced them to poor manners. It falls on me to thank you for being the agency which brought our family together once more.'

Robert was looking well. He had put on some weight, which was no bad thing in his case, and his clothes were of a very high quality. I noticed he had adopted the dubious habit of wearing jewellery. He almost looked too clean. In fact, everyone aboard the *Traveller*, except for Patrick and myself, looked like the cleanest people I'd ever set eyes on in my life. The boat itself was cleaner than we were. The decks looked and smelled freshly scrubbed. Even the sails shone with an other-worldly lustre. No livestock of any kind was housed on deck. I was amazed.

'This is a clean ship,' said Captain Cuffe, following my stare. 'Amongst our cargo to the Motherland you will find soap of all kinds and in great quantities; soap for the skin, soap for the hair, soap for glass, soap for wooden doors and tables, soap for flagstones and soap for clothes. Sierra Leone must not remain a place of disease and ignorance. It must be cleansed! Africa must be cleansed!' He paused and peered at us as if through a grimy window. 'And you too must be cleansed! Robert, take your brothers below decks. Give them pails of water, cloths and strong body-soap. They will wash before eating.'

* * *

The last time we had seen Robert he was waving us farewell from a London dock. He did not look too sad to see us go. In fact, he appeared downright eager to get back to work as an organizer for the gang of East Smithfield villains he was obliged to work for. Our last few days in London had been strange indeed. Our little brother, our so very clever little brother, was transforming in front of our eyes from a book-lover, a natural philosopher and cataloguer of every kind of phenomenon into an associate of highwaymen, a night-stalker, a lover of strong drink and a guest in the apartments of depraved women. We never doubted that we would see him again. As he never failed to point out, he was more intelligent than me. He was probably the most intelligent person I was ever likely to meet. But we could never have expected our paths to have crossed again in this way. 'Well, young man,' said Patrick, wiping tears of joy from his eyes. 'You have found us. You actually managed to do it! This is unbelievable! How did you get here?'

'I knew the *Boneta* was on course for Morocco. I had seen its instructions. It's what prompted me to leave London. It was an opportunity not to be missed.'

'You followed the ship in the hope of rescuing us?'

'Er, no. Not exactly.'

'You mean, you didn't know we were on board?'

'Nope. I did not check any ship's registers. For all I knew you were on your way home on board that merchant ship. I'm here because I wanted to get back home and also to see how the new machine, the new Turtle would function.'

'So you mean to tell me you travelled all the way from East Smithfield to get a glimpse of *that*?' he said, pointing through the hull in the direction of the Turtle as if it was dog mess. 'Why?'

'*That* is the most advanced form of military engineering in the world today. It is essential that we, as sons of Africa, should be witnesses to its operation.'

'Are you sure about that? Have *you* tried operating it? It's really not so advanced, is it, Jupiter?'

I seized my chance to jump into the conversation.

'What in God's name are you doing here, Robert?'

'Admiralty mail.'

'Sorry?'

'Admiralty mail.'

'I don't understand.'

'The mail. From the Admiralty.' My incomprehension caused Robert to shake his head in despair. I could feel my fists bunch. I was ready to strike him if he started his old chant: *Jupiter stupider*.

'The letters for the Royal Navy, that's what he means,' stated Patrick.

'Exactly. Remember how much money we owed those dockside criminals, the Franklin family?'

The memory was all too painful for me. My hot-headedness had put my brothers in great financial and moral debt to a gang of thieves. Patrick and I had planned on returning to Sierra Leone. Robert had volunteered to remain in London and work off our debt in service to the Franklins.

'In order to clear our debt to that set of rogues I arranged regular interceptions of some of the navy's mail. There was a local boy, an East Smithfield boy who worked as a messenger at the Admiralty. He'd give us the nod whenever mail would be passing through to the docks at our end or to the Kentish ports. Another local man was the coachman. It was all *very* profitable. We knew what was docking where and when and what they were carrying. We had sales of all sorts lined up weeks in advance.'

'And this messenger and the coachman: were they willing accomplices?'

'Far from it, but both had families. By the time I found out about Captain Cuffe's *Traveller* arriving I had paid off my debt and had made a fair amount of money on my own account. I was ready to leave. Besides, Cuffe is no stranger to Sierra Leone and I was correct in guessing that he was an acquaintance of our father. I paid him for my own passage home and I gave him additional monies to alter the *Traveller's* course to shadow the *Boneta's* convoy. Thus would we be protected from pirates and other rogues should we need a friendly flag to sail besides and it would afford us a slim chance of observing the Turtle in action from a distance.'

Before we could respond in any coherent way to what we were hearing, we were interrupted by Captain Cuffe shouting from the main deck. The order he had given was followed by a stampede of feet. We rushed up the hatchway to see what was happening.

'There!' the captain cried. 'No, over there. Behind those barrels. Mind the soap, I say. Over there! Sharply now!'

We joined the crew as they crowded around a pair of barrels lashed to a corner of the deck. Some of them carried brooms, one had a spade, another a mallet. They grew quiet, as if listening for something.

'What is it?' I whispered.

'One of Satan's emissaries. A rat. There can be no animals on this ship. *Kill him!*' hissed Cuffe.

'A rat, you say?' asked Patrick.

Cuffe huffed.

'Errrm, gentlemen, you cannot kill this rat.'

The crew looked at my brother as if he was a rat himself.

'You can't kill him. Not if it's who I think it is.'

'Not if it's who you think it is!' Cuffe roared with laughter and slapped his sides. 'You have stepped aboard this ship scant moments ago and already you are naming our pests?'

'I don't believe the rat is yours, Captain Cuffe. I think it came aboard with us from the Turtle. His name is Rupert.'

Patrick knelt down and peered between the barrels. 'Rupert? Ruuuupert? Here, Rupert. Over here, boy. You can come out. They won't hurt you.'

The rat hobbled out from his hiding place, zipped towards Patrick and ran up his arm to sit on his shoulder.

'What is that creature doing, travelling on your shoulder?'

'He is our new companion. We have experienced much together, haven't we, Rupert?' He scratched the rat under the chin. I am absolutely convinced the rat smiled back at him.

157

'What on earth have they been teaching you in the Royal Navy? Make sure that animal is either with you or locked up at all times. If I or any of my crew catch sight of it running free, it will die.'

[*15*]

'I trust you'll allow me to make detailed notes of your undersea experiences in due course?' asked Robert. Since we had renewed our acquaintance, our little brother seemed more pleased to see the submarine than to see us. We had a thousand questions for him, but he had no time for us. He passed the next three days studying the machine; cooing over it, tutting and fretting away inside it with his notebooks and sketchpads as it bobbed off the stern.

Patrick asked, 'Robert, you said you had money?'

'I have more, much more than money. Follow me.'

He led us into the darkest reaches of the ship.

'It's in there.'

He took a crowbar to a chest marked *Robert Williams Esq., Wilson St, Freetown, Sierra Leone, West Africa.* Inside, swaddled in cotton wool, were bottles of clear liquid. I pulled one out and worked the bung out of it.

'No! Don't put your finger in there! It burns.'

I sniffed. It smelled of nothing, yet left a burning

sensation in my nostrils.

'That's it, then? That's all you have from your time in London? This liquid fire?'

'It is vitriol of various kinds; nitric, sulphuric, hydrochloric.'

'And what use will this serve in Sierra Leone?'

'Our people need more than just bullets, Bibles and bread. We need our own manufactures!'

Patrick nodded approvingly.

'And what can we manufacture from this?'

'A great many things.'

'For example?'

'Errm, I'm not *exactly* sure.'

'And how much of it have you brought out of England. This liquid fire?'

'Several dozen gallons. It will be put to good use. Rest assured.'

The *Traveller*'s crew were no ordinary seamen. Although it did my heart much good to be on a vessel where beer and rum were not drunk more readily than water (in fact they drank no alcohol whatsoever), I confess I found Cuffe and his people disconcerting. For a start they behaved as if they belonged to some strange religious order. They dressed only in black and white. They prayed together upon rising and at midday, and at every meal, and at nightfall. They invoked the name of the Almighty in benediction upon the most ordinary circumstances; a favourable change of wind, a night of clement weather, the sight of a flock of birds or the setting of the sun. These men had an extraordinary hatred of dirt. They maintained fanatical levels of hygiene. Laundry was a daily affair and soap was used in almost industrial quantities. After a day or two it was all too much, even for me. The *Traveller* smelled, frankly, *girly*, and Patrick and I found ourselves longing for more vulgar companions. Despite their depravity and intemperate ways, Royal Navy hands are generally an amusing lot. They know how to have fun and can make the direst conditions bearable. The deckhands on the *Traveller* were as much fun as a gathering of Old Testament prophets. They hailed one another by declaring: 'Greetings, my brother,' and 'Hail, kinsman,' as if they had journeyed from afar bearing tablets of stone inscribed with commandments. On parting they always said, 'God be with you,' even if they were going as far as the head to relieve themselves. The instance of bad language I heard was: 'What in the blue blazes!' and this uttered by a man who had accidentally chopped off his thumb.

I grew to find conversation with them agonizing. Patrick, on discovering that a large part of the cargo was of Bibles and religious tracts, had as little to do with them as much as possible, preferring the company of Rupert.

We settled into our roles as paid-up passengers with great speed. On the third morning we had just finished breakfast and returned to our hammocks when a strained holler from the deck invaded our sleep. We heard the answering call of an officer of the watch. I was on the point of deciding this was no concern of mine and keen to rethread my dreams when the sharp whistle of a bosun's pipe sounded, followed by the captain's bellow: 'Hands make sail!' The vessel was suddenly alive with alarmed crewmen. Patrick and I were hauled bodily from our hammocks. Captain Cuffe and his first officer were on deck, ordering the crew through speaking-trumpets while peering at the horizon.

'Sail ho! Broad on our starboard beam!' cried Mr Kobena, the first officer.

'Aye, aye. I see her,' said Captain Cuffe.

A ship was within half a mile of us bearing hard on our starboard beam. I studied it through Robert's spyglass.

She was a strange-looking ship, long and laying low in the water. The combination of a huge curving lateen mainsail and a bank of oars on each side made her travel at a furious pace.

'They're pirates, sir,' Kobena declared. 'Corsairs. The ship is oared by galley slaves.'

The prospect of being captured by these brutes put fear into the strongest hearts. Looking about at the *Traveller*'s crew (proud and free men all), I knew they would fight to the death rather than live as galley slaves of the unbelievers.

'You can read the language of these heathens, Mr Kobena. What is the name of this ship?'

The first officer paused and focused his telescope more finely. I trained my glass along the side of the ship and saw a short line of writing that looked like a jumble of golden scimitars and minarets.

'It goes by the name of *The Blade of the Servant of Allah*, sir,' he reported.

'Does she indeed!' Cuffe harrumphed. 'Then this blade will be tempered in the flames of our Christian furnace!'

I looked along the deck to where the *Traveller*'s guns were being readied. There was no way on earth that our guns could match theirs.

'Do you Williams boys know how to hoist colours?' asked the captain.

'Aye, aye, sir,' we chorused.

'Then do so at once. Let the heathen know who they are up against.'

I jumped down to the flag locker and drew out the big ensign, bent it to the halyards and, with Patrick's help, ran it up the mizzen mast. Only as it fluttered freely did I realize that I had hoisted the Union Jack.

'But, Captain Cuffe, this is an American ship, is it not?'

'Aye, boy, it is and we are black men and Morocco is at war with the United States. We owe allegiance to no country save those in Africa, and until they have flags of their own we will sail under whichever ensign offers us the greatest convenience.'

I did not dwell too long on the absurdity of free black men sailing and fighting under white men's flags because a jet of flame and a cloud of smoke burst from the corsairs portside and immediately afterwards a heavy shot buzzed high over our mastheads.

The puny eight-pounder guns on the brig were run out and the three guns on the main deck replied instantly, but the shots fell short of the enemy vessel.

Although it was a brig, the *Traveller* was a

'perfect witch for speed'. It could change tack and turn like a gun on a pivot. A few sailors attending to the sails could change course in seconds. Before we knew it, our spars were covered in canvas and the *Traveller* was rushing away from the enemy, cutting through the water with a gentle, easy glide. The *Blade* fired a second volley towards us. It missed by a dozen yards or so.

'We can keep dodging and outpacing them for another two hours only. Then we must close with them and use our guns!' muttered Cuffe.

'But these guns are useless against them!' I shouted.

'The Lord shall make a way,' he intoned, fixing me with a glare that let me know exactly how much I had hurt his pride.

'Captain Cuffe,' Robert interjected. 'My brother is right. This is not a warship. Our situation is grave, the enemy is gaining on us and our time is limited. But if you'll allow me, I think I may have an idea . . .'

'This is no time for foolish talk. Either help out a gun crew or go below decks.'

'I would listen to him, if I were you, captain,' I said. 'We've nothing to lose, have we?'

'Indeed, captain,' piped Robert. 'I'll not get in the way, and will need only the help of my brothers to accomplish what I have in mind. And perhaps the temporary service of the ship's carpenter. We will be below decks for a while.'

Cuffe grunted his assent, perhaps more to get us off the main deck than anything else.

We stumbled off behind Robert.

'What are you thinking of doing now, boy?' asked Patrick.

'It's a new idea. A couple of fellows in London were discussing it . . . It might work . . .'

'*Might work?* What are you talking about?' roared Patrick.

'I'm not sure . . .' Robert scratched his chin.

'You're not sure! Well, you'd damn better well be sure. Where are you taking us, by the way?'

'To see the carpenter.'

'You want me to do whaaaat!' screamed the carpenter.

'Just eight barrels, I'm sure he won't miss it,' said Robert.

'He'll miss it all right. Eight whole barrels of soap flakes. He'll go crazy when he sees that's missing.'

'But it's only soap.'

'You don't really know him all that well, do you, young man?'

'I just need you to give us a hand. You can lever the lids off for us, then hammer them back on. It's not so hard.'

'And what else?'

'Oh yes. If you can get some strong yet supple wire, I'll need you to roll us a couple of dozen springs. And the barrels, they must be watertight. If not, then make them so. Oh yes, we are going to need a couple of dozen nails as well.'

The carpenter looked at our little brother as if he had lost his mind. In that same moment a shot from the *Blade* tore through the upper deck of the *Traveller*.

'You see, it really *is* a matter of life and death, sir.'

'What in God's name do you think you are doing?' Captain Cuffe stared unbelievingly as eight casks of his beloved soap were brought up on to the main deck.

'Please do not fret, captain,' said Robert. 'These barrels will save our lives. Besides, I will pay you for these items, in due course. If my idea works we will all live and our enemies will perish.'

'You are an odd child,' said Cuffe. 'Be about your business, but stay out of our way.'

I shunted the eighth barrel into position and

whispered to Robert, 'You said you would pay him for the use of his barrels.'

'I did, and I lied to him. I am penniless, as you know.'

'But what about the bottles of vitriol you brought from London. Surely you can exchange those to the value of his loss?'

'I cannot do that, Jupiter. I'm going to need those bottles for the next stage of my plan.'

'But, Robert. That is dishonest.'

He stared at me the way he always did before when he chanted: '*Jupiter stupider*', but luckily for him, he said nothing.

Robert refused to divulge any more of his scheme and demanded silence as we – Patrick, the carpenter and I – laboured.

First the woodworker got a small container of tar bubbling away and made each container watertight with fresh pitch. After that he set to work coiling the large number of springs Robert required. Patrick and I then followed his instructions to half empty each barrel of its contents. This part was almost fun, and we enjoyed flinging the stuff over the side, seeing the huge frothy wake we were making and sniffing the strange, almost sinister scent of briny perfume.

'This is the hard part now,' said Robert, 'and I must

do this alone. God pray this ship holds still.'

The *Blade* was still in sight, nearing us and taking the occasional ranging shot. The *Traveller's* crew performed their duties like magicians, dodging and turning from the larger craft with extraordinary skill. But that state of affairs could not last for ever.

The carpenter rejoined us. He attached each newly twisted spring to a large shipwright's nail, then gently tapped them into the barrels to the depth Robert requested. The poor man was next obliged to make fast a seal of pitch around all twenty-four nails.

At our little brother's feet was the chest full of bottles he was carrying back home. 'I'm going to need all of this,' he said with a voice seemingly choked with tears.

He had fashioned a rough pair of gloves for himself out of spare canvas, and he used these to lift out the large jars one by one, unscrew them and dribble their contents carefully into the waiting barrels. I noticed how, now and again, as the *Traveller* swerved, a tiny drop or so of liquid escaped the bottle and splashed on the deck. The wood smoked and holes were made where the acid fell. I could only wonder therefore at the effect of these chemicals on my brother's skin through the myriad tiny holes it had burned into his trousers. Robert was a brave and stalwart young fellow indeed, and my heart swelled with immeasurable pride to see him work on through these pains with undivided concentration.

At last all the barrels were ready.

'Captain Cuffe!' Robert called. 'I am going to need you to change tack twice more. Once so we can offload the casks and a final time to make good our escape.'

'But, lad, that will bring us almost right alongside them.'

'Yes, sir that is the idea.'

The *Blade* was now so close to us that we could hear the sinful din of galley slaves screaming amidst the cracking whips.

'Mr Kobena!' called Cuffe. 'Can our dear *Traveller* perform yet more manoeuvres?'

'That she can, sir!' snapped the first officer.

'Then on with your plan, Master Williams, and may God have His mercy on us all!'

One by one, we very gently rolled each barrel to the side of the ship. Once they were all lined up we tipped them, oh so carefully yet rapidly, into the sea to meet the prow of the oncoming *Blade*.

The pirate ship surged closer and closer and knocked into the first barrel in its path. Nothing happened. It audibly bumped a second, then a third cask to absolutely no effect whatsoever. Its looming prow pushed aside yet more barrels until it found itself surrounded by the redundant weapons. The *Blade* was now close enough for me to discern the grinning face of its prow-gunner brandishing a fizzing fuse and bringing it down to a bow cannon.

'Mr Kobena, change tack this instant. Change tack!' I hollered at the top of my voice.

The *Traveller* nipped aside, by mere inches this time, from the gun's blast and all on board knew there would be no second chance. The next encounter would be the last.

'Robert,' I said, 'what is supposed to be happening?'

'The *Blade* should have been destroyed in a massive explosion. It looks like the carpenter's springs weren't sensitive enough. Or something.'

'So. What are we going to do?'

'We'll shoot the barrels, yes!' he declared with a wicked glint in his eye. 'Captain Cuffe, some pistols, if you please!'

'Why, man, there are no personal firearms on board this ship!' He spread his hands. 'This is a Christian vessel. We are simple traders.'

'But you have ship's cannon to rake the enemy with

Christian flame, yet nothing to prevent your own men's capture should the vessel be boarded? Pah!' Patrick let out a scream of rage and went to fetch the two pistols we'd been given when we left the *Boneta*.

'Now, the trick is to get a shot straight through to one of the barrels. That should do it. That's all we need. One shot. Just one,' said Robert.

'Then that shot shall be mine,' I declared. I was always a better marksman than Patrick. I cocked a pistol, levelled it at one cask that rose and fell on a constant swell. If I timed the shot correctly, I would hit the target cleanly. I pulled the trigger. All that resulted from my shot was a reply from a host of small arms and muskets from the bow of the *Blade*. I couldn't believe I had missed! I never missed! *I never missed!* So consumed was I by my own failure that I did not see Patrick take aim with his firearm. I heard a click as he released the trigger, then the familiar light, wet fart of damp gunpowder. The pistol was useless. He hurled it to the deck and took cover from the barrage of shot coming from the enemy's decks.

As we hunkered down together, Robert held on to me. 'Jupiter, we have one last chance. It's all up to you. One last shot.'

'How do you mean? We have no more weapons.'

'Ah, but that's where you're wrong. Patrick, your slingshot, if you please.'

Robert took the slingshot and rolled across the deck to where the carpenter's brazier was cooling after heating the tar. Robert used his knife to scrape still-soft tar from the brazier and rolled it into a ball. He rolled across the deck a second time, to a gunner's mate now. I saw him receive a sprinkle of gunpowder and a lit fuse from the gunner's mate. He was back with us in a trice. The tar ball was rolled about in the gunpowder and the fuse, still alight and fizzing shorter was stuck into it.

'Jupiter, quickly now! Fling this on to a barrel!'

'Which barrel?'

'Any damned barrel! NOW!'

As this might be the last act I performed in this world, I stood my full height, heedless of the fact that I presented a perfect target for the *Blade's* small-arms men. As I swung the loaded slinsgshot, I angled myself towards the nearest barrel. I spun and let the missile fly. Up, over, out and across it flew, until it landed somewhere scant inches behind its intended target. I retook my crouched position and flung my arms around my brothers.

'Forgive me. I have failed, yet again. I'm sorry. Patrick, my only wish would have been that we had more time together, as family, I mean, and that you would have found the peace of God through Jesus Christ. And, Robert, you will—'

The *Traveller* was suddenly flung almost one hundred yards to starboard by the force of an explosion so great it threatened to roll it over through the waves. All the air was sucked out of my lungs and I felt my hair being singed as great sheets of flame roared against the side of the *Traveller*. The brig was pulled violently and just as suddenly in the opposite direction and for a moment those of us huddled against the starboard side were underwater. The boat righted itself quickly enough for us not to endure too much of a soaking. Shaking the water from ourselves like dogs, we peeked over the side to watch what was left of the *Blade* blazing away wildly on the horizon. It had been shifted an incredible distance. Another two explosions followed, one of which knocked the burning ship into the air only for the second to erupt underneath it and blow it all to matchwood.

'You did it, Robert! You did it!' I shouted. 'Praise be! Praise be! It worked.'

Mr Kobena, who had been sheltering from the blast

with us, wrung water from his neckerchief and asked, 'What in the name of all that is holy did you just do, boy? What was that?'

'I made some bombs,' chirped Robert. 'A number of water-borne bombs. But they didn't quite work. I don't know if that was down to the proportions in the mix or the quality of the springs, or the nature of the acids I introduced. I'll have to investigate that. They should have gone off as soon as they made contact with the ship's hull.'

'Robert, how do you know all of these things?' Patrick enquired.

'I read, Patrick.' He looked at our older brother oddly. 'Don't *you*?'

The captain walked over and embrace Robert.

'I should never have doubted you, boy. Truly, you were sent by God to take us through this time of trials.'

All night long and for much of the following day the crew of the *Traveller* celebrated their victory with barley water and prayers. And all through that day the sea ran red in places with the blood of the unbelievers and all of their Christian galley slaves.

[*16*]

Ah, Freetown!

After so long in the northern hemisphere, Sierra Leone looked like the most beautiful place imaginable. Seen from the bay, irregular streets stood on the banks of a large inlet of water and its houses gleamed white amidst gardens and trees. Handsome and extensive villas were scattered amongst the hillside. An extraordinary amount of vegetation of all kinds adorned the landscape. The soil itself, rich and loamy, could be smelled from a mile or so offshore. As we neared the harbour, I could see that the docks looked larger and busier than before. Not only were there new well-built stone warehouses, but a great number of ships from many lands were anchored there, or entering or leaving. Building work was going on all along the coast as far as the eye could see.

This was the view our parents would have seen as the ship that carried them (and me as an infant) from Canada came towards Africa. Mother and Father would have been about twenty-one or twenty-two back then. Only five years older than I was now. As always, it humbled me to reflect on their path through life. They had met and fallen in love while enslaved. Instead of living and dying as another's property, they had run away together and Father had served in the British Army during the colonial war in America. After the war, the two of them settled in Nova Scotia, Canada and, after many privations, they made it back to Africa, the Motherland. They were extraordinary people, and they were both dead. I wondered who would greet us in now Freetown.

It felt deeply odd to be back home. Even from the deck of the *Traveller* we could see there were a great many more European faces than we remembered. Not just sailors, but also soldiers were visible strolling about the harbour as if they owned the place. As we docked, a familiar rotting smell enveloped us. The stench was from the swamps and told of diseases which could enfeeble the strongest person not native to these parts. Mother died of swamp fever while giving birth to Robert.

There was a very large crowd teeming at the fence by the wharf where we docked. I had been away for almost four years in England and everything seemed very foreign. We had been for so long in the company of Europeans that we were shocked by the host of black faces before us. Not just the sheer number of them, but their *types*. Here were the people of our country, all of them! I immediately recognized those families most like our own; the soberly dressed, mild-mannered folk who (like Mother and Father) had settled here from Canada and had established themselves as a business class of sorts. Then there were the frank-featured descendants of the Jamaican Maroons, some of whom also lived amongst us as business people, administrators and teachers (though much more impressively dressed) . . . and everywhere, and in greatest number, like a class apart, the native peoples – the Mande, Temne and others, visible by their traditional dress or their badly tailored imitations of English fashions. But regardless of background, all Freetown had gathered to herald the arrival of Captain Paul Cuffe. And to a man and a woman they were singing the hymn 'Amazing Grace'. The passion and style of their rendition of what would have been a pretty dire hymn if sung in the traditional English style moved even Patrick to tears.

'We did it!' he sniffed. 'We made it. We are home, finally back home at last!'

We had barely stepped off the *Traveller* before

we found ourselves swept up in a fast moving crowd of people who had known us since we were babes. There were the Bannahs, the Gordons, the Naimbannas, the Princes, the Goodings, the Johns, the Booras, the Caulkers, the Peters, the Smiths and the Kizells. It was John Kizell, an old business partner of both our father and Captain Cuffe who fought his way through the mêlée and grasped Robert and me by the wrists.

By way of greeting he shouted, 'What are you doing here in Freetown? Why have you returned on this ship? You are supposed to be at school in London. Why have you returned? Do you know that your father is dead?'

While we recovered from this assault on our ears and manners he added, 'You will join me this evening for supper. Captain Cuffe will be there, also.' This was less of a suggestion than an outright order.

We said, 'Yes, sir,' and watched Mr Kizell claw his way through the rabble towards Captain Cuffe.

We attracted a swarm of well-wishers and the merely curious as we walked into town. I dimly recognized a few of those saluting and commiserating with us. Many were complete strangers. Without planning where our steps would take us, we arrived at the old Cotton Tree. The tree was in the very centre of Freetown. It was also where our mother had been buried. We looked in vain for Father's gravestone, but the hordes surrounding us prevented much movement in any direction and were by now a source of irritation.

'We will have a moment of peace with our mother, if you please!' Patrick begged the throng.

We stepped on to the tiny concession of ground the gawkers had cleared around her gravestone. With bowed heads we lost ourselves in thought and prayer, but my thoughts were not of our mother.

We were not there when Father died. None of us. Not me, not Patrick, not Robert. He died while Robert and I were studying at the African Academy in London and Patrick was in the hands of slave traders. Father had been murdered during a French attack on Freetown. The house had been burned to the ground, and presumably his bones with it. Although I know he must have died alone, I couldn't stop myself imagining him fighting off his attackers and dying surrounded by a retinue of faithful servants and friends. But he had no friends. There were never casual visitors in our house. Everything was business to him. He was a hard man. The servants hated him. If not a popular man, he was a good one. We owed him everything. We owed him a decent burial. I raised my head.

'Where is our father buried?' I shouted. 'Where do his bones lie?' There was no reply beyond a shaking of heads and much murmuring. The crowd seemed to be growing rather than diminishing. Only the presence of the large rat on Patrick's shoulder kept them at bay. Some of the less cultured folk stepped forward to feel our clothes and pat our pockets. I cuffed them aside and found my tongue well ready and able to lash them with a barrage of curses in local languages I had forgotten I ever knew.

Robert seemed quite overcome with all of this rough attention.

'Let's go home, shall we?' I suggested.

'Yes, let's go home. Take me home,' he asked Patrick in a voice I had not heard since he was seven years old.

The Williams family used to have several properties in and around Freetown. We had a house in the hills and a townhouse on Wilson Street, and a beach house for whenever we tired of company. Instinctively, our steps took us to the beach as it was furthest from the press of the town. I don't know what I expected to find but I was stunned to see the burned-out shell of a building that stood on there. I stepped over the broken gates and walked up the path overgrown with weeds. I kicked in a front door already half off its hinges and walked through the remains of the house I grew up in. A couple of pigs sniffed around in the hall and nibbled at the roots poking through the floorboards. The banister I used to slide down on a weekly basis was completely gone, as were most of the stairs. The walls of the drawing room and the kitchen where Patrick and I were taught to read and write had been knocked through to make a larger space for whoever was using the stove.

I walked into our old kitchen. A fire was still smouldering on the flagstones. An old woman sat to one side and poked at a bubbling iron stew pot slung above it.

I unleashed a torrent of bad language in several tongues until I determined that she was a Mande speaker. Patrick kicked over the pot and stamped on the fire. When I told her she had no right to remain there she emitted a terrible shriek and fell into spasms. All at once the house was alive with voices. We heard people charging from room to room and bouncing down the broken staircase towards us. A cloud of the old woman's enraged relatives burst into the kitchen swearing they would slice us up, dice us up and serve us with rice. Brandishing our unloaded firearms, Patrick and I commanded them in the rougher parts of the Mande language to go pack up their belongings and go elsewhere.

We made ourselves at home as well as we could amongst what remained of their rubble. We had not a penny between us, but we had each other and we had Mr Kizell.

Mr Kizell's house stood on the slope of a hill overlooking the harbour. Sea breezes blew through the open doors and windows. Polished floors of local wood and huge gilded mirrors would have made the rooms appear even larger than they were had it not been for the clutter of atrociously rendered family portraits, mounted pistols and other guns and the great many small tables full of regional art and knick-knacks.

The Kizells received us in the lofty, spacious apartment which took up half the width of the front part of the house. I sensed from my brothers' hunched postures that, like me, they felt weighed down by memories of the life we once enjoyed here: a life we could never reclaim. Mr Kizell in his manner and being was a strong reminder of our father. Like him, he had not just survived enslavement but had escaped it and made his way back to Africa where he had become a trader, preacher, property owner and so many other things that it made my mind swim to think on them. Once upon a time we had lived in a manner like this, in a house like this on a hill like this.

We were escorted to the verandah, shown to cushioned basket chairs and offered fresh lemonade with mint. The air was perfumed with the scent of a nearby herb garden. I had forgotten how fantastic the butterflies in this part of the world could be, how gorgeously plumed the birds were. Servants with towels and basins of warm water appeared. A feast of moin-moin, green-green, bush fowl and ground rice followed. We ate with our hands in the native manner.

As coffee was being served we were joined by a German missionary and an English naval engineer and his wife, all of whom were guests of the Kizells. Mrs Kizell seemed especially delighted to have Europeans under her roof, and she showed them off to us as if we had never conversed white people of such middling status before.

'Herr Ehlers, permit me to introduce the Williams boys: Patrick, Jupiter and Robert. They have returned from London only this afternoon. Isn't that correct?'

Patrick and I nodded our assent. Robert greeted the

German in his own language, whereupon they embarked on a brief conversation which caused Mrs Kizell to whoop with delight.

We were flattered to be included in the discussions between Captain Cuffe and Mr Kizell. I know I should have been enthusiastic about their talk of plans for a transatlantic shipping line run for and by people of African descent, but I was not interested in the least. I felt nothing but a growing strangeness sitting in this beautiful house and listening to the bare-footed padding of servants in the upper storeys as they drew and heated water for our baths.

After we had washed and changed into the new clothes supplied by our host, Mr Kizell gathered all his guests on front lawn.

'Now, my friends.' He spread his arms towards me and my brothers. 'News of your return will have spread throughout Freetown. The townspeople await you. Let us go to them that they may welcome you home. Let us go to worship in the house of the Lord!'

It was Tuesday evening.

A glance at Patrick confirmed that our hearts were both sinking at the same extraordinary speed at the mention of worship. We had been living amongst Europeans for so long that we had forgotten the meaning of worship in African society. Here churches are not just for Sunday. They are always open, and always full. I could never be described as a non-believer, but after all our adventures and losses I was genuinely exhausted and the last thing I wanted was to be trapped for up to four hours in a hot, stuffy church full of tambourine-knocking matrons and pious holders of public office.

Patrick's hands were bunched into fists and he stamped like a soldier as we made our way down the hill and through town to the Methodist church on Rawdon Street. Whilst in London he had revealed himself to be a fervent unbeliever. During his time as a slave he had had religion literally beaten out of him, he said. I shuddered to think what horrors this night would hold for him. Robert strolled along in front with the adults, merrily conversing on matters pertaining to international shipping and various treaties and alliances.

Patrick's face was a picture of tortured dignity as we entered the noisy little wooden building. Black people do not give praise in silence. A barrage of percussion and wailing assaulted us. Brightly dressed, bandanna-wearing women were swaying and jerking. Our arrival halted the service. We were suddenly surrounded on all sides by faces from our former lives. All the leading families were here; the Georges, the Goodings, the Nichols, the Peters, the Easmons and even our old enemies, the Cokers. Most of these people had been to England before on private business or on political delegations. Some of them had children who had been with us at the African Academy in London. They pressed themselves upon us asking for the latest news from London. Some of the girls from Mrs Dawes's school (who were looking very appealing, I must say) enquired as to my opinions on the current fashions in the capital. I am proud to say this is a subject on which my ignorance is perfect, but I was not above spinning out a little feeble fiction about French lace and cuff lengths to keep the young ladies in my orbit for as long as possible. Much to my alarm Robert appeared to possess not only considerable information about the state of men's and women's fashion in London, Paris and Jamaica, but he was also capable of giving the addresses of dressmakers and material vendors from these places. I vowed at that moment that I would read more often and widely in the hope of accruing benefits such as those my little brother was enjoying.

Patrick and I did not even try to join in the service. We were too tired to dance or sing.

The service recommenced with everyone holding hands. As both Mr Kizell and Captain Cuffe were ministers, each took a turn in leading. Captain Cuffe reminded us all to be sober and steadfast at all times, 'doing justly, loving mercy and walking humbly'. He called upon the younger members of the congregation to abstain from swearing, bad company and spiritous liquors and to discharge our obligations faithfully and industriously. Pointing at the native people looking in with their faces pressed against the windows, he ranted about their refusal to accept the blessings of the true faith and how they preferred the comforts of witchcraft and superstition.

I opened one eye and looked over the congregation. What a strange lot! Such publicly pious, white-worshipping, social-climbing people. They were who we would have become had we stayed in Freetown! All the same, we accepted an invitation to a party at the Kizells' the following evening.

Afterwards as we tramped back to our lightless beach house, Patrick dragged me away from our younger brother and hissed in my ear: 'Jupiter, have you not noticed? We don't have one single bank in Freetown, yet there are thirteen churches of all denominations and four mosques. How is that? Each of those houses of worship takes more of our people's money every Sunday than any bank could in a week. Why is that? Aaaaaaaargha!'

He flung his hat to the ground and stamped on it. I left him to his rage and watched him kick the hat down the dusty street all the way home.

We spent much of the following day arranging clothes for the party. In our tattered and stained outfits, we must have cut a sorry sight. There was little of a welcome and less credit for us at any of the general stores or outfitters. Our name no longer carried weight. Even invoking the names of powerful friends or old governors was to no avail. We were obliged to borrow clean, if ill-fitting clothes from the crew of the *Traveller*. Robert walked away with a gift of a few small coins.

The party was dreadful.

We were ushered in and introduced as if we were royalty. We were fussed over by hosts of old faces and encouraged to dance endless waltzes and minuets. I spent most of my time at the buffet stuffing my face with lobster, sweetcorn, pickled pork and rice. I swear I have never been amongst such a stuffy humourless set of people. Realizing I had absolutely nothing to say to any of these people, I put aside my customary disdain for alcohol. So I drank. Their punch, of course, was very poor stuff: strong in fresh fruit juice, but weak in alcohol. I chased the waiter around the ballroom and knocked back ten bumpers of the stuff. I would have finished off another ten if Patrick and Robert had not pulled me away from one of the Gooding girls. Apparently (I can't remember) I had requested her company on the verandah to take the night air. I had been naming points of light in the night sky when I launched myself at her. So I heard. I remember nothing of this, you understand. We stopped receiving invitations to balls after that.

Four nights later, Robert shook us from our sleep.

'I'm leaving,' he announced.

'What are you talking about, boy,' growled Patrick.

'I said I'm leaving. Going away.'

'How? Where? Why?' I asked, rubbing the sleep from my eyes.

'I am going with Herr Ehlers on an expedition down the Niger River. I will be his guide and translator. I know some German and quite a few of the languages used along the river down into Yoruba country.'

'Robert, are you sure about what you are doing?'

Patrick enquired. 'You do know what this man is, don't you?'

'A German?'

'No, boy! He's a missionary! He'll have you scaring those poor people with hellfire and damnation, and making them wear cravats and morning coats before they address strangers.'

'He is also an explorer. One of the best in the world.'

'What of it? Your job will be to safely deliver this white man into the heart of Africa. After him thousands more will follow, and they won't be carrying Bibles. Look around you. It's happening right here and now in Freetown. It won't be free much longer.'

'Jupiter, Patrick, I still must go. There's so much I have to see. And I can't continue living like this.' He pointed up at the stars shining through the gaps in the roof.

If I had learned one thing from my time abroad it was never to waste time worrying about my little brother. Robert would always prosper.

'Let him go, Patrick. He knows what he's doing, don't you, Robert?'

'I'm not sure, Jupiter. I'm not sure . . .'

We stayed up with him till daybreak. Then

accompanied him to the gates of the Kizell house where we bade him farewell.

'Hmmn. I was only just getting to know him,' Patrick rued, 'and now he's gone. I wonder what will become of him. He's so young.'

'Patrick, he's not the one I'm worried about! What are we going to do?'

'*We?* I'm staying right here in Freetown. No more travelling for me.'

'But won't you get bored? What will you do here? How are you going to live?'

'Jupiter, I can survive anywhere. But you forget, I'm the eldest. It still falls upon me to restore the family fortune. I must rebuild this house, then seek the restoration of remaining properties and start up the business again.'

'Where will you get the money to do all this?'

'The Turtle, remember?'

'You can't sell that. It belongs to the Royal Navy!'

Patrick shook his head. 'Oh, Jupiter, you don't understand. I can sell the machine to whoever I please. Any foreign power would be delighted to buy it.'

I was horrified by this turn of conversation. 'But you can't do that we . . . we . . . we're . . .'

'We are what? British? I think not. You're a good

man, little brother, too good perhaps. You've spent too much time with Mr Wilberforce and all those pleasant old men trying to stop the slave trade, but they're not the true face of Britain. The real face of Britain are those sailors and marines you see down at the new naval yard. They are not going away in the near future, believe me. They're here to stay, whether we like it or not. No. I don't owe Britain a thing. The way I see it, they owe me. Plenty. And the price for the Turtle should just about cover it, I think.' The prospect of this business brought an unusually cheery glow to his face. 'And you, Jupiter. What do the stars have in store for you?'

I would go mad in Freetown. Without the presence of our father, I was no longer part of this society and could never pretend to be. I had seen the outside world. I needed to see more.

'It's the navy for you, isn't it?'

'Perhaps,' I said. I imagined myself turning up at the naval yard and reporting for duty. I would be on a ship in no time at all. Maybe Captain Hibbert would keep his word and hold a middy's post for me.

I did really like the look of those uniforms. *Midshipman Jupiter Williams*. It sounded wonderful just saying the title.

'What do you think, Patrick?'

'I think you're old enough to make up your own mind, and what's more, you've done so already.'

Author's note

Although *Jupiter Amidships* is a work of fiction, it is based around a number of real historical individuals, events and situations.

Sailors of many nationalities served on Royal Navy vessels during the late eighteenth and early nineteenth century. African labour (both enslaved and free) in the Americas, the Caribbean, Africa and Britain itself led to the widespread presence of black sailors on British ships. Black men are recorded amongst all ranks from ship's cook to midshipmen and surgeons. A handful of them were commissioned officers and there seems to have been only one known instance of a black frigate captain (John Perkins on the Jamaica station).

Jupiter Williams and his family are very loosely modelled on the family of John Kizell. The Kizells arrived in Sierra Leone from Nova Scotia, Canada. In the late eighteenth century John had escaped enslavement to serve with the British Army during the American War of Independence. They became a leading family of traders and missionaries in the new settlement. A caricature of John Kizell appears in the pages of this book. Another caricatured figure is Captain Paul Cuffe. The African-American merchant, farmer and mariner Paul Cuffe was the wealthiest black man in North America at the turn of the nineteenth century. His brig *Traveller* (with its all-black crew) arrived in Liverpool in 1811 on its way to a three-month visit to Sierra Leone. Paul Cuffe and John Kizell became friends and business associates as described in the novel. For the purposes of *Jupiter Amidships* I have taken the liberty of having the *Traveller* sail in African waters some eight years before it would have.

The Turtle was the name given to the first submarine effectively fitted out for military use. It was designed by the American David Bushnell during the American War of Independence and used in a failed attempt to sink the British flagship *Eagle* in New York harbour in 1776. Bushnell is also credited with designing the first practical naval mine during the same period.

The settlement at Sierra Leone became a British colony in 1808.

In 1810 the Royal Navy imposed a colour bar which prohibited non-Europeans from becoming midshipmen,

ship's surgeons and officers. The colour bar lasted until
the 1960s.

Acknowledgments

Thanks are due to Inga Simmons for her hospitality and access to the fresh air of Whitstable where huge chunks of the narrative fell into place. Credit is also due to Peter Linebaugh, Charlie Foy and Marika Sherwood, whose research into naval history helped to flesh out elements of this text. Without the saintly patience of my editor, Beverley Birch, and all the editorial and production staff at Hodder Children's Books this book would not have been possible.

JUPITER WILLIAMS

S. I. Martin

Young, black, proud. Jupiter is boarding at the African Academy in Clapham with other wealthy boys.

But it's London 1803, and beyond Clapham lies another world, where poor black communities, slave and free, struggle to survive along the squalid reaches of the River Thames.

Into this world Jupiter's younger brother Robert vanishes, and there Jupiter must strive to find him . . .